**"Sometim<br>cheating Alex**

Easily pushing Alex's stroller with one hand, Nic took Cassidy's elbow in the other and guided them across the busy street. "Don't do that. Don't sell yourself short."

"I want what's best for him."

"That would be you. *You* are a real family. Small but mighty."

She was starting to believe him.

After they stepped up on the curb, Nic dropped his hold. She realized how protected and safe she'd felt for those few seconds. Nic was working his amazing charm on her and she couldn't seem to stop reacting to him.

He was in her thoughts constantly. And on the days he didn't bounce up to her apartment with some silly quip or tale of wild adventure or jokingly asking to borrow a cup of sugar, she missed him.

At times like this, she could forget he was a firefighter and how much that scared her.

Almost.

**Books by Linda Goodnight**

Love Inspired

*In the Spirit of...Christmas*
*A Very Special Delivery*
**A Season for Grace*
**A Touch of Grace*
**The Heart of Grace*
*Missionary Daddy*
*A Time to Heal*
*Home to Crossroads Ranch*
*The Baby Bond*

**The Brothers' Bond

## *LINDA GOODNIGHT*

Winner of a RITA® Award for excellence in inspirational fiction, Linda Goodnight has also won the Booksellers' Best, ACFW Book of the Year, and a Reviewers' Choice Award from *Romantic Times BOOKreviews* magazine. Linda has appeared on the Christian bestseller list and her romance novels have been translated into more than a dozen languages. Active in orphan ministry, this former nurse and teacher enjoys writing fiction that carries a message of hope and light in a sometimes dark world. She and her husband, Gene, live in Oklahoma. Readers can write to her at linda@lindagoodnight.com, or c/o Steeple Hill Books, 233 Broadway, Suite 1001, New York, NY 10279.

# The Baby Bond
## Linda Goodnight

Steeple
Hill®

Published by Steeple Hill Books™

STEEPLE HILL BOOKS

Steeple
Hill®

Recycling programs
for this product may
not exist in your area.

ISBN-13: 978-0-373-87528-3
ISBN-10:    0-373-87528-2

THE BABY BOND

Copyright © 2009 by Linda Goodnight

www.SteepleHill.com

Printed in U.S.A.

When you pass through the waters, I will be with you; and when you pass through the rivers, they will not sweep over you. When you walk through the fire, you will not be burned; the flames will not set you ablaze. For I am the Lord your God, the Holy One of Israel, your Savior.
—*Isaiah* 43:2–3

During the writing of this book, I was blessed to have the help of an awesome group of real-life heroes—the men of B Crew, Fire Station One in Norman, Oklahoma. Captain Lenny Mulder, Driver Keith Scott, and firefighters Matt Hart and Cody Goodnight answered any and all questions, discussed scenarios and even let me ride along on a call in the new fire engine. Thanks, guys. You're the best!

# Chapter One

Nic Carano leaped from the fire engine as soon as the truck came to a rolling stop, heedless of the sixty pounds of turnout gear weighing him down. Along with the captain, the driver and two other firefighters from Station One, he'd been the first to arrive on a very bad scene. Flames shot out of the front windows of an old two-story Victorian. Fully involved. Being devoured by the beast. Smoke plumed upward like gray, evil genies. With a sinking heart, Nic realized fire crews had only arrived and they were already behind.

Almost simultaneously, Engine Company Two wailed onto the scene and "pulled a spaghetti" as a pair of firefighters, moving in opposite directions, circled the structure with the two smaller lines.

Someone said, "We've got people inside."

Nic's adrenaline jacked to Mach speed. He glanced at his captain, and noticed the fire reflecting gold and red in the other man's pupils. Without a word, Nic tapped a finger to his chest. Ten minutes ago he'd been asleep in his bunk. Now he was wide awake and revved for takeoff.

"You and Ridge do the primary." Captain Jack Summers's graying mustache barely moved as he spoke. "No heroics."

His captain knew him well. Nic wanted in. He wanted to face the beast and win. Maybe he broke a rule now and then, but Captain knew he'd never endanger the crew. He and Sam Ridge, a quietly intense Kiowa Indian had gone to the academy together and practically read each other's minds.

If there were people inside, they would find them.

He and Ridge charged the house, pulling hose. Engine Company Two axed through the front door. The beast roared in anger. Nic and Sam hit their knees, crawling low into the dark gray blindness. As nozzle man, Nic went first, spraying hot spots while Sam rotated the thermal imaging camera left to right around the rooms.

The whoosh-hush of his own breathing filled his ears. *Darth Vader,* he thought with humor. Otherwise he heard nothing, saw nothing.

"Front room clear," he said, feeling his way through a doorway to the left and into the next room.

"We got casualties." His partner's terse words jacked another stream of adrenaline into Nic's already thundering bloodstream. He aimed the hose in the direction Sam indicated and crawled through the smoke to a bed. Two people lay far too still.

In moments, he and Ridge had shouldered the victims and were back outside. A man and a woman. Young. Maybe his age. He discerned no movement, no rise and fall of rib cage. Smoke, he figured, because they looked asleep. The woman was blond. In Scooby Doo pajamas.

Paramedics took over, working frantically. But Nic's gut hurt with the knowledge: they'd arrived too late.

Nic clenched his jaw against the emotion. Fury at the fire. Fury at himself for being too late.

Though he'd been on the force for five years and he'd been taught to stay detached, firefighters were human. This could be one of his sisters.

"I'm going back in," Nic said grimly. "There may be kids upstairs."

More victims was always a possibility. He could only hope the smoke hadn't gotten that far yet.

The captain gripped his shoulder. "Parrish and Chambers can go."

Nic shook his head, already changing to fresh air tanks. "Me and Ridge. We started it. Let us finish it."

The captain's radio crackled. Lifting the black rectangle to his lips, Summers motioned toward the inferno. "Go. Don't do anything stupid."

This wasn't the first time Nic had heard the warning. And it wouldn't be the last.

He and Sam made the stairs in double time. Fire danced below them, taunting and teasing. The firefighters outside were doing their job, knocking down the worst. Smoke rolled as wild and dark as Oklahoma thunderheads.

The thin wail of a smoke detector pierced the crackle and roar of the blaze. Downstairs had been ominously silent. No detector. Or one that had been disconnected. Nic's teeth tightened in sad frustration.

Again, moving clockwise, they searched two rooms before Nic heard another sound. He stopped so fast, his buddy slammed into him.

"Did you hear that?" Nic asked.

"Can't hear anything over that detector but you, puffing like a freight train."

Nic pointed with his chin. "Scan over there."

Sam raised the camera. "Bingo."

The noise came again, a mewling cry. "A kid?"

"Baby." Sam shifted the viewfinder into Nic's line of sight. "And he's kicking like mad."

Nic wasted no breath on the exultant shout that formed inside him. Handing off the nozzle to his partner, Nic approached the crib and had the crying child in his arms in seconds. His blood pumped harder than the engine outside, consuming way too much air. "Let's get out of here."

Sam scanned the rest of the room as they exited, hosing hot spots along the way. A crumpling roar shook the floor beneath them. They both froze. Nic tucked the baby closer, waiting to see if the flooring would give way and send them plummeting down into the inferno.

Sometimes Nic wondered if his afterlife would be like that: A trapdoor sprung open and a long fall down into the flames.

*Pray, Mama*, he thought, knowing Rosalie Carano prayed for him all the time. He was her stray son, the one who danced on the borderline between faith and failure. Often she told of waking in the night to pray when he was on duty. He hoped she'd awakened tonight.

With the fire below them, eating its way up, it was only a matter of time until the second floor would be fully involved or structurally unsound. If it wasn't already.

"Move it, Sam. This little dude is struggling." Everything in him wanted to break protocol and give the baby his air mask. He'd do it, too, if he had to and worry about the consequences later. Nic reached toward his regulator.

A gloved hand stopped him.

"Don't even think about it, hotshot," Ridge growled, reading his intention. "You're no good to him dead."

Ridge was right. As always. Neither of them knew what might transpire before they could escape. Firefighters had been trapped in far less volatile situations.

Nic gave a short nod and started down the stairs, the infant tight against his chest. Almost as quickly, he jerked to a stop and slung his opposite arm outward to block Sam. "Trouble."

Big trouble.

Heart jackhammering, Nic spoke into his radio. "Firefighter Carano to Captain of Engine One. Stairs have collapsed. We have an infant, approximately three months old, conscious and breathing, but we have no means of egress. I repeat, Captain, we have no means of egress."

A moment of silence seemed to stretch on forever. The baby had stopped struggling. Gone quiet.

*Pray, Mama. Pray for this kid.*

Nic was reaching for his air mask again when the radio crackled. "Firefighter Carano, you have a window on D side, second story. We'll send up an aerial."

He dropped his hand.

"10-4." Now to find the window. Fast. Though the upstairs smoke remained moderate, the darkness was complete. Without the imaging camera, he was as good as blind.

Keeping the baby as low to the ghostly haze as possible, Nic felt his way around the walls through the upper rooms, working toward what he hoped was D side. His partner found the exit first and opened it with a forcible exit tool. Glass shattered, the sound loud and welcome. The baby jerked. Cool night air rushed in.

Nic yearned to reassure the frightened infant. Through the plastic of his visor, he looked down into the wide, tearing eyes. Poor little dude would probably grow up with a terror of *Star Wars*.

The ladder clattered against the outside. Nic handed the child to Sam and climbed out, grateful for the flood of light as he reached back for the baby. He always appreciated life and light and fresh air a lot more after an entry such as this.

In seconds, he was down the ladder and on the ground.

Paramedics whisked the baby out of his arms and started toward the ambulance. Nic followed, ripping away his helmet and mask as he walked.

His legs felt like deadweights inside his turnout boots.

"He gonna be all right?"

The red-haired paramedic, Shannon Phipps, nodded, her busy hands assessing, applying oxygen and otherwise doing her job with rapid-fire efficiency.

"You done good, Carano," she said.

Nic knew he was expected to shoot back a wisecrack so he did. In truth, all he could think of was the tiny boy in blue sleepers who would never know his mother and father.

"We'll get him to the hospital," Shannon said. "But I think he'll make it. Listen to that cry."

Nic nodded, watched the paramedics load and slam doors. Heard the *whack-whack* of a hand on the back indicating the ambulance could pull away.

He jogged to his captain, equipment thudding, and then, as the ambulance started to leave, he stepped in front of the headlights. The driver slammed on his breaks and rolled down his window.

With a frown, the paramedic said, "Carano, I should have known it was you. You maniac, what are you doing?"

"Make room," he said. "I'm going with you."

*This can't be real. This can't be real. Please, God in heaven, this can't be real.*

Cassidy Willis's mind chanted disjointed prayers and denials as she stumbled down the corridor of Northwood Regional.

Janna and Brad would be waiting for her. They would laugh and yell a very cruel "April Fool." This was not real. Her sister and brother-in-law could not be dead.

A nurse stopped her. "Miss, are you all right?"

Cassidy nodded numbly.

"Fine." The word came out as a croak. "I need room twelve-fifteen. Alexander Brown. My nephew."

Comprehension and a heavy dose of compassion registered behind the nurse's glasses. She knew baby Alex was an orphan now.

An orphan. Oh no. Could she live through this torment again? She'd already lost her parents. Janna had been her family, her best friend, her sister. They'd had each other when life had been too hard to bear.

Cassidy closed her eyes and swayed. The nurse looped an arm gently through hers. "I'll walk you down. You must be devastated."

Devastated. Devastated. Like a recording stuck on repeat, words reverberated and replayed in her head.

All she could do was nod and stumble on, going through the motions. Doing what had to be done.

Whatever that was.

Alex. Baby Alex needed her. He was alone. All alone in a violent world that had stolen his mommy and daddy. A mommy and daddy who had loved him fiercely.

She felt lost. Alone. Just like Alex.

At the door of the room, she paused and sucked in a deep breath, hoping for strength, settling for vague sensory input. Hospital food. The clatter of trays coming off the elevator. Breakfast.

It seemed like hours since the sheriff had appeared at her door. But morning had just arrived, the dawn of a new and terrible day. A day she could not bear to face.

Maybe she was still asleep. Still dreaming. That was it. Bad dreams about death and destruction were all too common to her.

*Wake up, Cass. Wake up.*

The urging didn't work. She was still standing outside a

thick, brown door inside Northwood Regional Hospital staring into the gentle eyes of a nurse. Wishing she could slide to the floor and die, too, Cassidy faced the fact that this nightmare was the real thing.

"Is Alex…?" How did she ask if he was horribly burned or hooked up to tubes and wires? If he was suffering?

The nurse nodded, understanding Cassidy's concern. "He was far enough away from the fire to escape the worst. He suffered some smoke inhalation, but nothing that breathing treatments won't resolve in a few days. He should recover well."

With a push to the center of her glasses, the kind woman left the rest unsaid. Alex had slept in the remodeled nursery upstairs. His parents slept downstairs in the unfinished portion of the old house. The fire must have started on the bottom floor, sucking their lives away while they slept, exhausted from the chore of remodeling the beautiful old Victorian into a bed-and-breakfast. A dream that would die with them.

The nurse hovered, leaning close to whisper. "He came in with the baby. I hope you don't mind."

Cassidy paused, perplexed, the flat of one hand against the cool wooden door.

"Who?" She had no relatives close enough to have arrived already. Not anymore. No one but Alex.

"The firefighter. He won't leave."

Cassidy tensed. The last thing she wanted was a firefighter hanging around to remind her of what she and Alex had lost this horrible night. She wanted the man to get out, to leave her in peace. But she hadn't the strength to say so.

"I'll handle things from here. Thank you." Her voice sounded strangely detached, as though her vocal cords belonged to someone else far away in a big, empty auditorium.

"If I can do anything…."

Cassidy managed a nod. At least she thought she did as she pushed the door open and stepped inside.

The eerie quiet that invades a hospital deepened inside the room. Pale morning light from the curtained windows fell across a bulky form. Still dressed in the dark-yellow pants and black boots of a firefighter, stinking of soot and smoke, a man had pulled a chair against the side of Alex's crib. Turnout coat hung on the back of the chair, his dark head was bowed, forehead balanced on the raised railing. One of his hands stretched between the bars, holding Alex's tiny fingers.

Too exhausted and numb and grief-stricken to think, Cassidy paused in the doorway to contemplate the unlikely pair—a baby and a fireman. What was the man doing? Sleeping? Praying? Why was he here?

Unexpected gratitude filtered in to mix and mingle with her other rampaging emotions. After the night's tragedy, she could hardly bear to think about anything related to fire—even the men who fought it—but she was very glad her four-month-old nephew had not been alone all this time.

The fireman roused himself, lifting his head to observe the sleeping baby and then to turn and look at her. Cassidy's first impression was of darkness. The same black soot covering his clothes smeared his face, so that Cassidy had a hard time discerning his age or looks. His eyes, though reddened behind the spiky eyelashes, were as dark as his nearly black hair. Only the fingerprint cleft in his chin stood out, stark white against the soot.

With another look at the baby, the man carefully slid his fingers from Alex's grip and stood. He wasn't overly tall, but his upper body was athletic and fit beneath the navy Northwood Fire Department shirt. Weariness emanated from him.

"Are you the aunt?" he asked. "They said he had an aunt." He glanced back at Alex, swallowed. "My sister has a baby."

Then he stopped as if the word *sister* was too strong a reminder of the night's loss.

"Yes, I'm his aunt. Cassidy Willis."

She moved to the raised crib and gazed down at the child with her sister's dark-blond hair and Brad's high cheekbones. What was she going to do now? What would Janna want her to do? Who would be mother and father to her sister's little boy?

"Is anyone else coming to be with you?"

Gripping the rail with both hands, she struggled to think. Her brain was a fog. Her emotions jumbled, but mostly numb.

"Brad's parents."

"Brad?" he asked gently, standing close as though he thought she'd faint. The scent of smoke seeped from him in insidious waves. Her stomach churned, fighting down a memory. She'd hated the smell of smoke before. Now she hated it even more.

"Alex's father. My sister's husband, Bradley Brown."

"Ah." He didn't have to say the words. She could hear his thoughts. Brad Brown was dead along with her sister.

"His parents live in Missouri, just over the state line. They'll come."

"Have they been notified?"

She looked at him then, lost. Notified? Of what? "The fire?"

"Yes, ma'am."

"I gave their information to the sheriff." At least she thought she had. Those moments in her small living room with the solemn sheriff were a painful blur, a slow-motion torture of trying to comprehend the loss, of answering questions, of understanding that Alex needed her and she had no time to grieve.

She knew little about Brad's parents except that they lived in Joplin and had raised a son who loved her sister. The pair of them had been building the one thing Janna and Cassidy had always dreamed of—a real family.

"The sheriff will make sure they are notified."

Good. She wasn't certain she could speak the words that resigned her sister to eternity. *Dead* was such a powerful term, as if saying it aloud made it so.

"They're probably on their way now. My grandmother. I called her." For whatever good it would do.

Grandmother Bassett had been detached from her life and Janna's, an austere provider who sometimes seemed surprised to find them living in her house. She'd taken them in as orphans, but she'd been too busy with her business and her own social circle to be a parent. Though a good person in her way, Eleanor Bassett did not know how to comfort and nurture. If she came at all, she'd do so only to issue orders.

With a shudder of hopelessness, Cassidy realized she had no one now to understand and share her pain. No one to help her make decisions for Alex. No one but God. And at the moment, God seemed far, far away.

*Oh, Janna. My beloved sister.*

"Isn't there someone close? You shouldn't be alone."

She'd always had Janna. They'd run to each other when trouble came. "No one, but I'm fine."

For most of her life, she'd depended on no one but Janna or herself. Leaning on others, asking for help, did not come easily. She could handle this, the same way she'd handled the loss of her parents and growing up in a home that was less than warm. Without God, she wasn't sure she would have survived to adulthood. This time, the burden was almost too much to bear.

Her body sagged. She crossed her arms in an attempt to remain upright.

The firefighter touched the back of her shoulder. "I could call someone for you. You need your family."

He had no idea. She opened her mouth to reply that she had

no family now, but she would be all right. He should go away and leave her alone. Leave her to think things through, to figure out where to go from here.

Baby Alex chose that instant to stir. Both adults turned their attention to the crib. Dressed in a hospital gown decorated with yellow ducks, he looked small and helpless. Murky blue-brown eyes blinked up at Cassidy. She touched his reaching hand and felt his strong grip against her fingers. Her heart turned over with love and regret.

"He doesn't seem to have suffered any permanent effects," she murmured, more to herself than to the fireman.

"He's a tough one. A fighter." The man reached inside the crib again as though he couldn't keep his hands off the tiny survivor. Alex kicked his feet, happy with the attention. "His eyes are still red. They were streaming from the smoke when I brought him down."

"You?" Of course, now his presence made sense. She turned slightly, caught the hint of emotion in the man's face. This close, she could see he was about her age and was probably nice-looking beneath the grime. "You rescued Alex."

Which meant he must have seen Janna and Brad, too. She wouldn't ask about that.

"Handsome little dude." His full bottom lip curved.

As if insulted, Alex's small face puckered and he began to cry. Cassidy reached inside the crib and lifted him into her arms, thankful that he was not attached to the wires and tubes she'd feared.

He cried louder. She bounced him up and down, feeling as helpless as he did. She was his aunt, not his mother. What did she know about soothing a baby? She'd spent time with him, but Janna had always been nearby, ready to take over when the crying commenced. It had been a standard joke between her and her sister. Cassidy played with Alex. Janna did all the hard stuff.

"It's probably breakfast time, don't you think?" the fireman asked.

Oh dear. Breakfast. Cassidy's stomach fell to her toes. "I don't know what to do."

He shot her an odd look, as if everyone knew what to do with a hungry baby. "Give him a bottle, I guess."

Cassidy bit her bottom lip, both embarrassed and dismayed. "Janna was nursing him. He's never had a bottle."

In fact, Janna had never left her son with anyone, not even Cassidy, for more than a few minutes. Alex was her child of joy and promise, the beginning of the big family she and Brad had wanted. If Cassidy was honest, Janna was living the life both sisters had longed for.

"Oh. That does present a problem." He held up one finger. "Sounds like a job for the nurse."

He pushed the button and issued the order for formula as though he did this every day. Maybe he had kids of his own.

"Thank you. I hope Alex can deal with the change," Cassidy said, juggling the fussy child up and down, up and down, praying the nurse would hurry with that bottle.

"It may take some time, but he will."

He must be a dad, she thought. Nice guy, firefighter, baby expert. Not hard to look at, either. Interesting fellow. "I never did get your name."

"Carano," he said. "Nic Carano. Fire Station One."

Cassidy blinked. He couldn't be. No way. This firefighter who had rescued her nephew was Nic Carano?

Notorious Nic?

## Chapter Two

"I remember you," she said, trying to reconcile the helpful firefighter with the Notorious Nic she remembered.

He'd dated half the girls in her sorority house. All at once. Nic Carano, the fun-loving life of the party who went through girlfriends faster than frat boys through a keg of beer. She'd been very careful to be sure she wasn't one of them.

Nic was not her kind of man. If she had a kind. Unfortunately, building her career in graphic design left her little time to date. If she did, it would not be a man like Notorious Nic, no matter how nice-looking and charming he seemed.

The door swished open and a nurse attired in blue scrubs appeared with a bottle, patted Alex's head and disappeared again. As if she had a clue what she was doing, Cassidy tilted the baby into a cradle hold and slid the nipple into his squalling mouth. Alex shoved back, twisting his head, fighting the strange silicone.

"You look familiar to me, too." Apparently unperturbed by Alex's crying, Nic went on talking as he pushed a chair behind Cassidy's knees. Gratefully, Cassidy slid onto the seat. She hadn't realized she was still standing. "College maybe?"

Cassidy nodded. "Kappa Kappa."

"Oh yeah." He grinned. "My favorite sorority. You lived there?"

He asked as if he were puzzled, as if he hadn't dated her so how could she have lived in the Kappa Kappa House.

For one thing, she'd been too focused. For another, she'd been too smart to get involved with a man who was all charm and no substance. Though loath to admit it, her social life had been limited to a few shallow, quickly fading relationships, a couple of them regrettable. The Lord had forgiven her, but she was taking no chances on making the same mistakes again. Handsome, charming, shallow men were off-limits.

Alex grew frustrated and thrashed in howling protest. Cassidy jiggled the bottle, trying to calm him. She'd had no idea feeding a hungry baby could be this difficult.

"Come on, sugar. I know it's different, but you'll get the hang of it."

She tried again, sliding the nipple onto his tongue. He jerked away, pushing at her hand.

"Want me to try?" Nic held out his arms. "I've got a little experience."

"You do?" Now that was a shocker.

He winked. "Trust me. I'm amazing."

Right. Trust him. How many girls had heard that line? Trusting Nic was the last thing on her agenda. In fact, the sooner Fireman Fun and Games disappeared, the better. She had enough to deal with.

"I appreciate all you've done, Nic. Really." She jiggled Alex harder. "But you must be exhausted. I can handle things from here. You look like you could sleep for a week."

Alex screamed, a cry that would bring police, and fire and rescue in any other setting.

Fire and rescue was already here, holding out his arms, with a funny little quirk at the corner of his mouth.

If Nic comprehended her efforts to get rid of him, he didn't show it.

"Come on. Let me try. Me and the little dude are buddies. I can sleep when I'm dead."

The word *dead* lingered between them, harsh and dark. The night's tragedy slipped back into the room. As though water flowed through her veins instead of blood, Cassidy's arms went weak.

What was she going to do without Janna? What was Alex going to do without a mother who knew how to soothe him when he cried?

"Hey," Nic said, his voice soft and concerned. She raised her eyes to his and he must have seen her helplessness. Without asking again, he took Alex from her.

Cassidy sat, limp and devastated, trying to think of anything except that ugly word—*dead*. Her head was like an echo chamber bouncing the word back a thousand times. *Dead, dead, dead.*

Swallowing a cry of anguish, she focused on Nic Carano, cradling her nephew against his chest as if holding a baby was the most natural thing in the world.

Did that mean Nic Carano was now married with children? That the wild and crazy jokester without a care in the world was not only a firefighter, he was a dad?

The image didn't fit. The party boy she remembered did not have either "responsibility" or "settle down" anywhere in his vocabulary.

Right now, however, he was using his charm to convince Alex to accept the unfamiliar bottle. He pressed a dab of formula onto the infant's lips and then stroked the corner of his mouth with the nipple. As if by some form of communication known only to the male species, Alex turned his face and latched on.

"Attaboy," Nic murmured. His gaze flicked up to Cassidy's. "Look at him go."

Cassidy should have felt better. Instead, her depression deepened. If she couldn't even feed Alex, how could she care for him? And if she didn't, who would? She was no more parent material than Nic Carano. Nor did she possess his natural ease with people.

"How did you do that?"

Nic shrugged. A small smile gleamed white against his dirty face. "Told you," he said easily. "Uncle Nicky's got the touch."

"Are you this good with your own kids?" she asked, not because she cared about his life one way or the other, but to keep from thinking about Janna and Brad.

Nic drew back in feigned alarm. "The Caranos have enough rug rats running around the place without me adding to the numbers. I'm *Uncle* Nicky. Not Daddy Nic."

That sounded more like the Nic she remembered. Naturally he would love to play with the little ones, but he wouldn't want to take on such a responsibility. The guy probably still lived at home so his mom could do his laundry.

"No matter where you learned, I appreciate your expertise. I'm kind of lost."

Lost and more afraid than she'd been since that night in the Philippines. And almost as helpless.

Shoulders sagging, she closed her eyes. Janna's pretty face laughed behind her eyelids.

Somehow Nic managed to hold Alex and his bottle as he leaned toward her, stirring the sickening stench of smoke. "Are you sure you're gonna be okay?"

Cassidy nodded, numb and empty. She would never be

okay again, but what could Nic Carano do about it? What could anyone do?

"I'm sorry." He tilted his chin toward the baby. Alex gazed up at him with wide, earnest eyes, still sucking for all he was worth. "Sorry for both of you. I wish there was something more I could do."

What good was sorry? She was sorry, too, but Janna was still gone. There were no words to describe how shattered she felt, how special Janna was or how much both she and Alex had lost last night.

Insides chilled, Cassidy drew her crossed arms tightly against her body as if to ward off reality. She longed to go to sleep, wake up tomorrow and discover this had all been a bad dream.

"Where do you go from here?" Nic asked gently. "I mean, who's going to care for the little dude?"

The "little dude" had finished off his bottle. As if handling a baby was second nature, Nic set the bottle on the floor, lifted Alex to his shoulder and patted his back. Alex made gurgling, satisfied noises, oblivious to the drastic change in his life.

"I don't know what we'll do." She didn't want to think about the future. She could barely deal with the here and now. "Brad had no siblings and there was only Janna and me in our family." She thought about Brad's parents. They might be willing to raise Alex.

"My sister's a social worker. She might be able to help."

The idea of a social worker frightened Cassidy.

"No," she said a little too sharply. "No social services."

She trembled to think of her nephew growing up lonely and unloved the way she and Janna had. Alex deserved a loving home and family, not a parade of foster homes. She would choose. She would make the decision. Somehow.

"Forget I brought it up. Today is way too soon to think about that."

"I never dreamed this would happen to Janna," she murmured.

"No one ever expects a tragedy of this magnitude. Not even us firefighters. These things happen to other people. Not to us. Or so we think."

Almost to herself, Cassidy said, "I don't understand why God would let this happen."

*Again*, she thought. Twice in her life she'd lost those closest to her. It wasn't fair. She'd always considered God to be a good and loving God, the Father she'd lost as a child. Now she was left floundering to understand. Had she failed in some way? Was she being punished?

"You got me there," Nic said. He tapped Alex on the nose and waited for the toothless smile before settling him on his lap to face Cassidy. Alex made a goo-goo sound, waving his arms in poignant happiness as he recognized her. "My mom would say all things work to the good for those who love God, but I have to admit I don't get the whole God thing."

Cassidy, too, was having a hard time believing that anything good could come from the death of two young, caring, godly people and the orphaning of their son.

"So you aren't a believer?"

His smile was crooked. "Oh, yeah, I believe."

Cassidy heard the unspoken "but" at the end of his proclamation, though she didn't understand it.

From her missionary parents, she'd learned to love, revere and serve God all the days of her life. Regardless of her questions, God was the only answer. He was her anchor, her only hope. Though she couldn't begin to understand, she had to believe God was with her. The alternative was hopelessness. How could anyone face an uncertain future without His strength and courage to sustain them?

She was about to ask Nic that very question, when he crinkled his nose. "Uh-oh. Change time." Averting his head, he pushed the baby in her direction. "Uncle Nic does not do diapers."

His lighthearted comment was a welcome diversion. She smiled in spite of herself.

"Firemen are supposed to be brave."

He made a face. "Brave is relative. Give me a nasty, dirty fire any day, but not a nasty, dirty diaper."

A nasty, dirty fire. Nic's words brought back the pain, as sharp and plunging as an ice pick. She wished he would go away. He was a walking, talking reminder of death.

She'd had enough of death to last a lifetime.

Holding Alex, she abruptly stood, turning her back on the gear-clad firefighter. "Thanks for all you've done, Nic. I'll take it from here."

Her words were a stiff dismissal he couldn't possibly miss this time.

A moment of silence stretched behind her. She didn't turn around. If she did, she would apologize, and he would stay longer. He had to go and take his ghoulish job with him.

"If you need anything—"

Why did he have to be nice? "I won't. Bye, Nic."

She was giving him the brush-off?

Nic shifted on his feet, his boots heavy, his body weary. He wanted to be ticked, but he tamped down the reaction. Cassidy Willis was living a nightmare he couldn't begin to comprehend. She looked so shattered that for a minute or two there, he'd been tempted to take her in his arms and comfort her. With most women, he would have done exactly that, but the classy-looking blonde exuded a cool aloofness that kept him at bay. For some reason, she wanted him to leave, but he couldn't do that, either. Not yet anyway.

Normally, he didn't get involved with fire victims, but last night the baby boy had gotten to him in a big way. As he'd waited in the emergency room, the child had clung to him, calm only as long as Nic was present and touching him. The little dude seemed to intuitively understand that his parents were gone and that Nic had saved his life.

Then when the aunt had stumbled into the room, the soft heart that sometimes got Nic into trouble had done a weird flip-flop, like a banked bass. Compassion, he supposed, but he was intrigued, too, though he had to admit, all women intrigued him. Ladies were a gift from God. Might as well enjoy them. But Cassidy Willis was different from his usual lady friends. Perhaps not in looks—she did have those—but in demeanor.

He'd known she was the aunt right away. She resembled the woman in the Scooby Doo pajamas he'd carried out of the burning house. Only where Alex's mother had been dark-blond, Cassidy's hair was sleek platinum, the kind that required considerable maintenance. Pampered sorority girl hair that went perfectly with her fancy acrylic nails.

She also had the kind of blue eyes men dream about, as vivid as his mama's pansies. At the moment they were filled with anguish.

She must have been heading out for a jog when the news arrived because she wore a running outfit. From the looks of her slim form and pro athletic shoes, Cassidy Willis was a serious runner.

Too bad she couldn't run away from the situation. Her world had turned upside down and she was coping pretty well, he thought. Well enough to want him to leave.

He was kind of offended at that. Most women wanted him to hang around. This one wanted him to leave.

In any other situation, he'd consider that a challenge.

Maybe he did anyway.

Her back still turned as if he wasn't in the room, Cassidy

reached beneath the crib, found a box of baby wipes and a clean diaper. He should go. He needed to go. Hanging out in hospitals with orphaned babies and bereaved women wasn't his idea of a party.

Still, he felt this *obligation* to do something for her and the little dude.

Cassidy's polished beauty was right up his alley, but her looks were the farthest thing from his mind. He wasn't after a date. He had a couple of those already. He was after—Nic didn't know for sure what he was after.

For reasons he could not explain, he couldn't walk away and forget this pair. He should. He wanted to. But something irrevocable had happened last night and he couldn't live with himself if he didn't do s*omething* for them. Besides, his big, pushy family would have his head if he didn't look after a damsel in distress.

Maybe that was the problem. Family expectations, as usual, were his undoing.

"Hang on," he said, though she clearly wasn't leaving and had effectively shut him out. "I'll be right back."

He jogged out of the room, only to reappear in seconds bearing a pen and notepad. The nice nurse at the desk had been all smiles and obliging. He grinned and patted his chest with the flat of one hand. Must be the uniform.

He scribbled on the sheet, ripped off the page and handed it to Cassidy.

"Here you go," he said. "That's my cell and my house. Call if I can do anything."

The way Cassidy stared at his broad scrawl made Nic wish he'd taken more interest in penmanship.

"Thanks." She pocketed the piece of paper without enthusiasm.

"I'm serious," Nic said, backing toward the door. "Call. I have a whole army of family who'd be glad to help."

She nodded but returned her attention to the baby.

It wasn't the reaction Nic was hoping for, but he'd done his duty. His conscience could rest. He needn't give Cassidy Willis another thought.

Maybe.

## Chapter Three

Nic met the angular, suit-clad woman in the hallway coming in as he was leaving. When she stopped at the nurse's desk and asked for Alexander Brown's room, Nic knew she must be the grandmother Cassidy had spoken of. A sense of release settled over him. Cassidy and the baby needed this woman's company.

Coming from a very large family, he couldn't imagine having so few relatives. In fact, he'd tried to imagine it a few times but with the Carano bunch, he never had a moment's peace. They were in his business more than he was. At times he resented them for that, but situations such as this one made him appreciate the circle of love.

Which did not mean he wasn't going to move out on his own as soon as he found an apartment. No matter how his parents argued that it was not necessary. No matter how economical the arrangement might be, no matter how expensive apartment rentals were, Nic needed his own space. Space to study for another go at medical school exams. Space to be away from the prying eyes and pressure of second-generation Americans who expected him to be something more than what he was. Much as he loved them, a big family could be trying.

With a quirk of his lips, Nic admitted to himself that he would, however, miss his mama's cooking.

He was pushing the elevator button when he heard the older woman ask in a high and nasal voice, "Has anyone telephoned child welfare? That baby will need to be adopted out."

He pivoted for a better look at Cassidy's grandmother. The woman looked as though she had swallowed a glass of vinegar and was sorely annoyed to be in this place. Not grieved, annoyed.

Maybe he'd been wrong about Cassidy needing her family.

He squeezed the bridge of his nose with his thumb and forefinger, thinking, fighting the temptation and losing so fast his head spun. He needed to head home, clean up, catch some Zs. He and Lacey and Sherry Lynn were on for a Redhawks game tonight. This was none of his business. Cassidy didn't even want him here. She'd practically tossed him out on his ear.

But baby Alex had wanted him, and the little dude was the one in jeopardy.

Besides, as Nic and his firefighter buddies always said, he could sleep when he was dead.

With a tired sigh, he headed back down the hall to the baby's room, knowing he was about to stick his nose where it did not belong. Mama would say he was going to get it cut off one of these days.

The thought put a spring in his step.

The never knowing when was part of life's adventure.

With the flat of his hand, Nic pushed open the door to room twelve-fifteen and followed the vinegar woman inside.

Cassidy turned from the crib in surprise. Her gaze slid past her grandmother to him. "Nic. I thought you'd left."

"I did."

She patted Alex's back and covered him with a blanket. "Did you forget something?"

"Yeah."

She glanced around the small room. "What is it?"

He ignored the question. "Is this your grandmother?" *And did you know she wants to put Alex up for adoption?*

Vinegar lady slid a critical glance over his dirty face and uniform. Her nostrils twitched in distaste. "A fireman, I presume?"

His mama would throttle him if he was rude to his elders. Vinegar lady didn't know how lucky she was. "Yes, ma'am. Nic Carano. I'm a friend of Cassidy's."

Cassidy's eyes widened at the word *friend*, but she didn't deny him. "Nic, this is my grandmother, Eleanor Bassett. Grandmother, Nic rescued Alex from the…house."

Again, Mrs. Bassett settled narrowed blue eyes on him. The blue eyes were about the only thing she had in common with her granddaughter.

"Thank you, Mr. Carano." The gratitude seemed to pain her.

"Nic," he said. Poor Cassidy, if this was her comforting family, she was in a world of hurt. The woman hadn't so much as hugged her.

"I suppose the Browns have been notified." Mrs. Bassett perched her narrow backside on the edge of a chair and folded her hands atop an expensive-looking handbag. Dressed in a business suit the color of zucchini, she appeared ready to conduct a board meeting. *Or*, Nic thought with a hidden grin, *be chopped into a salad. Add a dab of oil to the vinegar and voilà, lunch.*

"Yes, Grandmother." Cassidy's face, so pale before, was now blotchy red. "They've been notified."

If he was a guessing man, he'd say vinegar lady made her granddaughter both anxious and unhappy.

She was starting to do the same to him. Nic Carano did not like to feel either of those emotions. The woman needed an injection of fun. Or cyanide. The bit of internal sarcasm tickled him. He would laugh later.

Mrs. Bassett checked her watch. "They should be arriving soon. If I can drive from Dallas, they should be able to get here from Joplin in equal time."

"They've lost their only son, Grandmother."

"Yes. A shame, too. Bradley was a good boy. That wind is awful today. My hair's a mess. I'll have to call Philippe for a recomb." She patted the brown fluff around her face. "There are so many details to take care of. I hope they arrive soon. I have a dinner party tonight. We need to get the problems ironed out today."

"Well, I certainly wouldn't want you to miss a dinner party on the day of your granddaughter's death." Cassidy's words were quietly spoken, but the resentment was clear. So were the red splotches covering her cheeks and neck.

What had he walked into? And why didn't he hit the road before the war broke out?

One look at Cassidy, standing sentry beside Alex's crib, hands white-knuckled against the railing, gave him his answer. She was fighting to hold herself together, as much for her sister's baby as for herself. Aunt Cassidy needed his support, whether she wanted it or not. Baby Alex needed him even more.

"Don't be sarcastic, Cassidy. It isn't ladylike." Vinegar lady opened her purse and removed a card. "This is my attorney. He can help work out the details."

Nic crossed his arms and leaned against a wall, glad to have some plaster to hold up his fatigued body. Cassidy glanced his way as if just remembering he was there. Something flickered behind those baby blues. He gave her a wink of encouragement. She glared back, clearly not wanting him to stay. Call it macho, call it stubborn, but the notion made him even more determined to stick around.

"I don't know what you mean, Grandmother." Cassidy

took the card, studied the face, turned it over and then back again. "Why do we need a lawyer?"

"Issues of estate. The problem of Alexander."

Cassidy's hackles rose. She stood up straighter. "Alex is not a problem."

"You know what I mean, dear. He'll need new parents, although the Browns may have some notion of taking him on."

Taking him on. That's the way Grandmother had thought of her and Janna, as unpleasant responsibilities she had incurred. The notion would have hurt if Cassidy hadn't always known.

"No," Cassidy said with surprising firmness. "Not strangers."

"Be reasonable, Cassidy. The child is still young enough to be acceptable to adopters."

"I don't want someone to take him because he's acceptable. I want him to be loved."

Grandmother huffed; her mouth puckered tighter. "I was afraid you'd be like this. You and Janna could be so stubborn at times, binding together in your fits of determination."

Trembling with fatigue and emotion, Cassidy pressed a hand to her forehead. A dozen issues she'd never considered or discussed with Janna filtered through her head. The only thing she knew for certain was that she, not Grandmother, needed to make this decision. She prayed she was strong enough to stand against the powerhouse woman whose iron hand ran a company with several hundred employees.

Nic, whom she'd almost forgotten, surprised her by pushing off the wall and coming to stand beside her. He brought the nauseating scent of smoke with him. Why had he come back when she'd been more than clear that she neither needed nor wanted his interference?

He took one of her hands. She knew she should yank it away, but she was too weak and empty to fight both Nic and her grandmother. When the firefighter gave her fingers a squeeze, she realized how cold she'd become since Grandmother's arrival. How sad that a virtual stranger—even one she didn't particularly like—could provide more comfort than her own flesh and blood.

Considering that painful fact, maybe Grandmother was right. Perhaps adoption was the answer.

She pulled her hand away, knotting it with the other in front of her. Nic's eyes bore into the side of her face, but she kept her gaze trained on Alex.

*Dear Lord, help. My mind is so scattered right now.*

As though someone had asked for his input, Nic said, "You need some time to think. Nothing should be decided today when you're still in shock."

Grasping that tiny bit of good sense, Cassidy nodded. He was right. She was running on fumes and emotion. How could she make an intelligent decision about Alex's future in this condition?

Grandmother did not agree. "The sooner you settle things, the better. You have a busy career and Alexander has nowhere to go. I am simply not up to taking on another child."

"Grandmother, please," she interrupted before Eleanor could begin her diatribe on the supreme sacrifice she'd made when Cassidy's parents died. Cassidy was determined that Alex would never feel the sting of believing he was an intruder living in someone else's home. She wanted better for her nephew and with God's help, she would figure out something.

Eleanor had opened her mouth to say more when Beverly and Thomas Brown entered the room. Both of them looked completely shattered. Cassidy rushed to greet them.

"I am so sorry," she said to Brad's mother. "I don't know what else to say."

The matronly woman fell against her with a sob. "I can't

believe this. I kept hoping we would get here and discover some kind of ghastly mistake had been made."

Hadn't she prayed for the same thing?

Thomas, a portly man, stood by looking helpless, his jowls droopy with sorrow. "How could this have happened?"

"I don't know," Cassidy said honestly. "I suppose the fire marshal will investigate."

She glanced at Nic, amazed that he hadn't left. He nodded and extended a hand to Thomas. "Nic Carano. I was at the scene last night."

"Did you see them?" Beverly, eyes puffy and red, pulled away from Cassidy to face the fireman. Her short brown hair, shot with gray, was in disarray as if she'd run her hands through it over and over again in her distress. "My son and his wife?"

"Yes, ma'am. I brought them out."

"Are they certain of the identities?"

The heartbroken mother was grasping at straws, hoping for a miracle that would not come. Cassidy's stomach rolled, sick with grief.

"I don't know about that, ma'am, but I can assure you they died peacefully and easily in their sleep. Smoke inhalation. No pain. No suffering. No fear."

Thomas clapped a huge paw onto Nic's shoulder, mouth downcast, as he drew in a shuddering breath and then nodded once. "Thank you for that. It helps."

The atmosphere ached with sorrow.

"Yes, sir."

"Nic rescued Alex, too," Cassidy said, glad for the first time that Nic had returned to the room. His professional ease and knowledge of the situation seemed to be exactly what the devastated Browns needed.

"Thank you, Nic," Beverly said and hugged him. The firefighter embraced her as if he'd known her forever. No surprise there. Nic Carano was comfortable with people, especially women.

Cassidy's grandmother had kept her peace for about as long as she could. "We need to plan services, I suppose."

The other four turned to look at her. Perched on the chair like a queen on her throne, Eleanor would run the show or die trying.

Somehow Cassidy stumbled through the visit to the funeral home, the preparations for the services and the double funeral four days later. In the midst of making all sorts of arrangements and decisions she hadn't realized were necessary, she'd warded off Grandmother's attempts to "deal with the issue" of Alex until after the funeral.

She and the Browns had taken turns sitting with the baby at the hospital where they'd discussed the painfully few options for her nephew, but none of them were emotionally ready to make a permanent decision.

To Cassidy's discomfort, Nic Carano had returned every day as well, sending the baby into an excited display of arm and leg pumps and slobbery smiles. Cassidy, on the other hand, suffered a pain the size of Dallas. Every time she saw him, she had an unbidden vision of the yellow-clad fireman carrying Janna from the house, limp and dead. He was too much of a reminder of that night, of her sister's last hours and moments.

Out of uniform, he looked different, more like the wild and crazy Nic in funny T-shirts she remembered. She couldn't understand why he kept coming around. Surely not to see her. Having had her fill of womanizing playboys, she'd let him know from the start that she was not interested.

Alex was the only explanation. Through the shared tragedy, Nic had bonded with the child. That's all it could be.

Until today, the doctors had kept her nephew in the hospital for observation and respiratory therapy. Two hours ago, he'd been discharged into Cassidy's care—temporarily.

Now on this pleasant April afternoon, she sat on the off-white sofa in her tidy living room with Alex asleep in her lap, feeling as if she were a house of cards, ready to tumble at the slightest breeze. The grandparents were on their way to make the decision.

"Oh, baby boy," she whispered to his peaceful, innocent face. "What is going to become of you?"

Earlier, her pastor had stopped by with a word of counsel and a prayer for comfort and guidance as she made important decisions in the days ahead. He'd prayed for Alex, too, that God's will and perfect plan would unfold. To her way of thinking, God's perfect plan should have been Janna and Brad raising their son together. Yet, she'd found relief in Pastor John's prayers. Since the accident, praying had been difficult.

Heart as heavy as it had ever been in her life, Cassidy dreaded the family meeting that would decide Alex's fate.

A bitter laugh escaped her throat.

"Family," she muttered with a shake of her head. "Some family you have, baby."

Beverly and Thomas Brown were fine people, but Beverly's heart wasn't strong. She'd had two bypass surgeries already. They couldn't raise an infant and had admitted as much, though they loved Alex with all the grandparent love in the world. Eleanor, thank goodness, had never even considered "taking him on." Had she wanted Alex, a moving freight train could not have stopped her.

Grandmother wasn't a bad person, just a focused, determined businesswoman who'd never forgiven her only daughter for marrying a penniless missionary and then dying in a "heathen" land. Janna and Cassidy had borne the brunt of her unforgiveness.

With a shudder, Cassidy made up her mind that her nephew would never live that way. She wanted him to have love and family and warmth and support. A dear cousin in Baton Rouge was interested in adopting Alex, but Louisiana seemed so far away. Cassidy wanted him nearby, close enough that she could be part of his life.

If only she were married or had a less demanding job. If only she possessed the natural mothering instincts of her sister. If only her future weren't laid out before her like a tidy road to the top of her game.

But it was. Regardless of the crazy thoughts going through her mind every time she looked into Alex's face, she had no business raising a child.

"Lord," she whispered, smoothing her fingers over Alex's velvety forehead. "Show me what to do. Make Your plan clear. I'm dreadfully confused."

Grandmother had declared today the final day she would "worry" about this situation, because she had business to attend to. Though Cassidy had urged Eleanor to return to Dallas and let her and the Browns decide, Grandmother wouldn't hear of leaving until the issue was settled.

"I take familial duty very seriously," she'd insisted with an insulted sniff. Behind her back, Cassidy had rolled her eyes.

Someone pounded on the door. Cassidy jumped. Baby Alex jerked and threw his arms out to the side but didn't wake.

"They're here, lamb," she told him, stomach churning to know that after today, she would be separated from this baby she'd loved since before his birth.

Having no crib, and worried he would roll off the sofa, Cassidy placed Alex on a blanket on the floor, and then went to the door expecting to find the Browns or her grandmother waiting.

Instead, the handsome face of Nic Carano grinned down at

her. In a snug black T-shirt imprinted with "Slackers give 100%, just not all at once," he looked firefighter fit and beach tanned.

Cassidy's stomach fluttered in a troubling and inappropriate response.

"Hey," he said, slouching against her door.

Charm absolutely oozed from the man.

"Nic?" Her voice was cool to the point of frost. Maybe he'd get the idea. "What are you doing?" *And why won't you go away?*

"Went by the hospital to see the little dude and they said he'd escaped with a beautiful blonde."

She refused to fall for the compliment. It rolled from his silver tongue far too easily. "I brought him home this morning."

"I called the sibs." With a jerk of his thumb, he indicated an oncoming barrage of humanity. "Told them a friend needed some baby stuff and here they are."

A parade of people she didn't know had piled out of cars and were trailing up the sidewalk like smiling, supply-laden ants. Each carried something that related to an infant.

Cassidy was dumbfounded. "They're bringing those things for Alex?"

Oh dear. What did she do now?

The dimple in Nic's chin widened. "Unless you wear Huggies and onesies and play with bathtub toys." He shook his head, one hand up to wave off the remark. "Scratch the last comment. Everyone needs a rubber ducky."

Against her own better judgment, Cassidy laughed. "Nic, you're a nut."

With a cocky grin, he turned and hollered down the stairwell. "Come on up, folks. She's laughing. I don't think she'll shoot."

While Cassidy wrestled with the wisdom of letting Notorious Nic into her house, a ribbon of chattering, jostling Caranos, all toting various baby items, trudged up the steps and into her space. Nic stood in the doorway like an affable traffic cop, rattling off introductions as three men and three women passed through. Even with six, Nic declared that some of the family had to work today.

"These are only the goof-offs," he said with affection.

Cassidy, confused, touched and annoyed in equal amounts, could only watch in stunned amazement. How many Caranos could there be? Where did they get all this stuff? Why would they give it to her?

A man Nic introduced as his father, Leo, paused in the living room to ask, "Where do you want us to put everything?"

With his blue-collar physique and thin ring of hair around a shiny bald head, Leo Carano would have been perfect in a sitcom set in a pizza parlor.

"Anywhere," she said, and then, discombobulated, changed her mind. "No, wait. The guest bedroom."

What was she doing? Alex wasn't here to stay. The furniture would only have to be moved again.

Before she could tell them as much, a beautiful, full-figured woman reminiscent of Sophia Loren stopped with a box of baby clothes in her arms.

"I'm Rosalie," she said, hitching her chin toward Nic. "This rascal is my baby boy."

No wonder Nic was so handsome.

"Now, Mom," Nic said with considerable humor. "Don't start telling stories."

Rosalie cocked an eyebrow at him. "Then stop lazing in the door and go help your brothers. Cassidy won't remember who was who anyway. Later, we'll get acquainted. Anna's bringing pizza."

Pizza? Somehow she had to stop the madness and tell these people that she could not accept their generosity. Alex was not here to stay.

A painful knot formed in her throat.

"Nic," she started.

"Gotta go," he said, cutting her off.

With a parting wink, he saluted his mother before bounding down the steps. On the way, he shouted general insults at his brothers. They shouted back, all in good fun.

Cassidy watched in fascination at the family dynamics. Teasing, working together, the bond of love between them was practically visible. Her heart ached with the knowledge that this was the kind of life Janna and Brad had been building for Alex. Now what would he have? Where would he go?

Rosalie returned from the bedroom, empty-handed. "I think my Nicky likes you."

Liked her? No way. "He likes the baby, I think. He rescued him from the fire and they seem to have formed a bond."

It was the only explanation she could think of, the only acceptable one.

"Precious angel from God." Rosalie looked over at Alex who didn't seem to mind that an army of Caranos were tromping all around him. "You'll be a fine mother for him, I'm sure."

"Oh, I can't keep him. That's what I've been trying to say."

The woman was taken aback. "I'm sorry. I thought Nic said you were the aunt, the only sister of the baby's mother."

"I am. It's just that…"

Rosalie tilted her kind face to listen. Cassidy stumbled through her litany of reasons.

"I've already missed four work days. I can't keep a baby. I'm single. I don't know anything about babies. My job is demanding. I'm working my way up to creative director. That's even more demanding. Alex deserves…" Realizing she was babbling, Cassidy clamped her lips together.

Rosalie patted her arm. "It's all right, Cassidy. Alex deserves love. Everything else is negotiable."

Cassidy opened her mouth to say more but nothing came out.

"You'll do the right thing. God will guide you."

She hoped she could count on that.

"But what about all these lovely things? I can't keep them."

The woman waved her off. "As long as you need them. We know where they are." Then Rosalie stuck her head out the door and called down the stairs. "Come on, boys. This baby does not need to sleep on a floor with all of you tromping around like Bigfoot. Bring that up here."

Two men who looked remarkably like Nic pulled a baby crib from the back of a pickup.

Cassidy felt a moment of panic. This was getting out of control. Did she need a crib?

One of Nic's dark-haired sisters, Mia, if she remembered correctly, asked, "The baby is awake. Do you mind if I pick him up?"

"No. Please. I—" Cassidy blinked, as confused as a minnow in a whirlpool.

Her heart continued to race as load after load of baby paraphernalia, much of which she could not identify, found its way into her apartment. By the time the pickup and two cars were unloaded, the guest room was crammed with baby items.

With relentless cheer, the Caranos went to work organizing and setting up. The men clanged away at the crib, arguing over the direction of the springs and screws. The ladies folded sweet-smelling clothes and placed them inside a small chest.

The Caranos were like a tidal wave, overwhelming in their power. Cassidy gave up the battle. She'd deal with this later.

"What is this thing?" Nic asked, holding up a device with a dangling electric cord.

"Baby wipe warmer." Mia's full lips curved in amusement at her clueless brother. "Now that my little one is out of diapers I don't need it or most of this other stuff. Thank goodness."

"Sweet," Nic answered and found a place for the warmer on the baby changer. "Right here okay, Cass?"

No one called her Cass.

"Perfect," she muttered, helpless to say otherwise.

Nic efficiently filled the machine from a package of wipes, plugged it in and then wove his way through the maze of working Caranos and baby stuff to her side.

Smelling like baby wipes, a fact that made Cassidy want to giggle, the macho fireman plopped down on the floor and tilted a roll of Life Savers toward her.

She was on her knees next to Rosalie sorting onesies by size. "Overwhelmed yet?"

She dug a cherry candy from the wrapper. "A little."

"Want us to disappear?"

What could she say? To tell the truth would be both unkind and lacking in gratitude. Suspecting she would live to regret the decision, she said, "Stay."

"Sure?" He popped a lemon Life Saver into his mouth.

Trying not to remember who he was or his role in her sister's death, Cassidy controlled the urge to send him away. She slid the candy onto her tongue and sucked at the sweetness.

During the hour since the Caranos had swept into her life with their friendly laughter and kindhearted intentions, she'd pushed aside the terrible circumstances that brought them here. For this little while she'd witnessed the inner workings of a real family, the kind she and Janna had dreamed of. For the first time since Janna's death, she'd felt almost human. That's why she'd let them stay. She'd needed to feel normal again.

Now the sorrow came back in a rush.

Nic was silent beside her as though he guessed her thoughts. Guilty, troubled, hurting, she folded and refolded the onesie, never taking her eyes off the tiny garment.

*I'm a mess.* She, a woman who had long known what she

wanted and where she was going, now floundered like a baby bird fallen from the nest.

The intrusion of a single, high-pitched, nasal voice jolted Cassidy from her brooding.

"What is all this?" Eleanor Bassett stomped into their midst, the heels of her alligator pumps thudding ominously on the beige carpet. Beverly and Thomas Brown peeked in behind her. Ignoring them, Grandmother swept one arm imperiously around the bedroom filled with boxes, diapers, bottles, a changing station, a crib and a lot of people.

Nic leaned into Cassidy's ear and whispered, "Cruella de Vil. Hide the puppies."

Squelching a gust of sudden and surprising laughter, Cassidy pushed at his shoulder and stood. He came up with her, eyes dancing above an expression as innocent as a rose. He'd probably gotten away with a lot of things because of that face.

"Grandmother, come in. I'd like you to meet the Carano family." She'd almost added "friends of mine" and yet she hardly knew them. This amazing group that had baffled her with their display of generosity to a bereaved aunt and an orphaned baby were basically strangers.

Introductions were made and Grandmother perched on the rocker, ready to take over. The Caranos, while polite, didn't seem all that impressed.

"Cassidy, we've come to discuss the situation. Although I see no reason whatsoever for you to have purchased all this frippery, shall we adjourn to the living room and leave these people to their work?"

The Caranos exchanged amused glances, aware they had been relegated to the position of hired help.

"Grandmother, the Caranos are friends." There. She'd said it. "They donated these items for Alex."

"Oh. Well." Eleanor tilted her nose down a notch. "Unnecessary given the situation, but thank you. How generous. Now, Cassidy, as I was saying, let's adjourn to the living room. I need to get back to Dallas tonight. The Forkner merger is set for tomorrow and I have tons of paperwork to prepare."

Cassidy looked from the woman who'd birthed her mother to Nic's sister who held Alex. The blue-clad baby reached chubby arms toward his aunt. Cassidy's heart swelled with an undeniable emotion—love. Her knees started to shake. Could she do this? Could she let Grandmother ship him off to virtual strangers? Could her heart let him go?

The answer came loud and clear. No. She could not.

*Lord, help me.* She was about to jump off a building without a safety net.

"Grandmother. Mr. and Mrs. Brown." She sucked in a steadying lungful of Nic-scented air and let it out slowly. This was the right thing. The only thing. "I want to keep Alex."

Nic squeezed her elbow.

Buoyed by that simple gesture and the growing confidence that no one else could love Alex the way she would, Cassidy took her nephew from a gently smiling Mia and kissed the top of his head. His warm baby smell filled her senses and settled in her heart.

"That's ridiculous, Cassidy. You have no business with a child. You have a busy, growing career."

That was one of the dozen problems she hadn't figured out—yet.

"Something will work out."

"Well now, if that isn't a well-considered plan." Grandmother's nostrils flared in sarcasm. "You're single, Cassidy. You cannot raise a child and that is all there is to it."

The Caranos had grown quiet, eyes averted as they busied themselves with work, trying not to listen. All but Nic who stood at her side like some kind of warrior, which was ridiculous given that this was Notorious Nic. Despite his job, Nic wasn't a fighter. He was a player.

Still, his solid presence was oddly strengthening. She, who had rarely won a battle with Eleanor Bassett, quelled the trembling in her bones.

"I promised Janna and Brad."

"Promised them what?" Grandmother's mouth puckered. Vertical lines, like spokes in a wheel, circled her lips. "To give up your own life?"

Cassidy's chin rose a notch. She could feel the red blotches creeping up her neck. She hoped Grandmother didn't take them as a sign of weakness. She was anxious, not weak.

"I promised to take care of Alex if anything should ever happen to them." With the stress and confusion of the past few days, she'd forgotten the conversation and the piece of computer-printed paper until this moment.

"Oh, for goodness' sake." Eleanor waved at the air in dismissal. "No one would hold you to some silly, sentimental promise."

"I would. I believe God would, too. Janna and I knew from experience that the worst could happen. She loved Alex so much, she wanted to be certain he would never—" She stopped before she could say too much. Her grandmother had tried. Hurting her now had no value. "We even put her wishes in writing with the nurses as witnesses. I have the paper in my safe-deposit box, if anyone wants to see it."

The day after Alexander Bradley Brown was born, Brad and Janna had handed her a document asking her to act as legal guardian if anything should ever happen to them. She'd wanted to laugh it off, but she and Janna knew that life didn't always play fair.

"We think it's a wonderful solution, Cassidy," Beverly Brown said, coming close enough to stroke Alex's hair. Tears filled the woman's eyes. "This is what we've prayed for, though we didn't want to pressure you. You're young and healthy, and you love this baby."

"You'll always be his grandparents," she said, aching for Beverly's loss. "He'll need you in his life."

"Thank you, honey," Beverly whispered. "We want that very much."

Without a word, she slid Alex into his grandmother's arms and watched her cradle the infant tenderly. Tears shimmied loose and slid silently down the woman's ruddy cheeks.

Grandmother Bassett, however, was determined to have her way. "You're running on emotion, Cassidy Luanne. This can't last. Then later, you will be sorry you made such a drastic mistake."

With a sharp pang, Cassidy realized Grandmother spoke from experience. She considered taking Janna and Cassidy into her home a "drastic mistake." That final, cruel comment gave Cassidy the last bit of courage she needed.

"Loving Alex could never, *ever* be a mistake."

Regardless of her single status, regardless of the demanding career, regardless of her goal to be a premiere graphic designer, and though she knew nothing at all about raising a baby, Cassidy Willis would find a way to give her sister's son the loving home he deserved.

# Chapter Four

Nic tossed down the remote, skirted the semicircle of recliners pointed at a television set and headed into the kitchen area of Station One to dish up the lasagna. Four tough, manly firefighters followed like puppies. Tonight was his night to cook at the fire station, and thanks to his mother's recipes, Nic's cooking was favored by the other men.

"Not as good as your mama's," Captain Summers teased, his mustached mouth so full his words were mush. "Passable."

Above high cheekbones, Sam Ridge's brown eyes glittered with amusement, but he said nothing. Such was Sam's way. If he strung twenty words together during a twenty-four-hour shift, everyone sat up and listened. Nic always figured he and Ridge got on so well because Nic liked to talk and Sam liked to listen. Pretty sweet deal.

The Kiowa took an extra slice of buttered garlic bread, lifted it toward Nic in appreciation and returned to his chair to eat and watch reruns of *MASH*. If they were lucky, no calls would come in before they'd finished their meal.

During Nic's rookie year, Mama had appeared at the fire station to supervise the kitchen on his night to cook. Now that Nic had the recipes down, Mama still came around on occasion with pastries or breads from the family bakery. The other men lived for the times Rosalie Carano swept into the station to see "her boys," as she called all of them.

Lately Nic wished Mama wouldn't come around so often. Though he laughed at the good-natured teasing, the mama's boy comments were growing thin.

Nic dished up a healthy dose of steaming, cheesy casserole, his belly whimpering in anticipation. Other than a few medical calls, a couple of motor vehicle accidents and a grass fire, today's shift had been slow, both a blessing and a pain. Nic liked to be busy. Taking care of the station, the engines and the equipment was part of the job as was ongoing training, but he liked the adrenaline rush of a callout.

From the corner of his eye, Nic caught movement at the outside door. A luscious brunette, long hair blowing in the fierce Oklahoma wind, swept into the station. Behind her came a short, perky redhead.

*Ah, well,* he thought with a grin, *there are other types of adrenaline rushes.*

"Mandy! Rachel!" Nic said. "What's going on?"

One of the cool perks of being a firefighter was that citizens could drop by any time. Even gorgeous girl citizens who only came in to flirt.

He could deal with that.

Rachel, the leggy brunette, swept her hair back with one hand. "Came by to see you, what else?"

From the circle of recliners came the usual hum of interest. Sam and the other firefighter, "Slim Jim" Wagner, momentarily lost interest in Nic's lasagna.

Mandy, the perky redhead, opened a tiny purse and extracted a brochure. "We're getting up a group to go to the beach. Are you game?"

Trips to anywhere entertaining were right up his alley.

After a long, windy and cold winter, some fun in the sun sounded pretty sweet. "When?"

"This weekend." She waved a photo of blue water lapping at sunny, white-sand beaches. "Three days at a friend's condo right on the beach in Galveston."

This weekend. He'd planned to drop by and check on Cassidy and Alex this weekend. Not that Cassidy was all that hot to see him. Fact of the business, he'd called her a couple of times since she'd made the decision to become Alex's permanent guardian, but she never answered the phone.

Weird.

He hoped she didn't have caller ID. The implications of that would be ego-crushing.

She'd sent cards to him, his parents and siblings expressing gratitude for their help. Nic would have preferred a phone call. One of those gushy-breathed, "Oh, Nicky, thank you so much for being there for me and baby Alex." But what did he get? A formal card with all the warmth of January.

He must be losing his edge.

He thought she liked him okay, but he also felt a kind of pushing away, as though she was too polite to say so, but she didn't want him around.

A terrific, fun-loving guy like him, he thought with humor. What wasn't to like?

Rachel's voice intruded on his aberrant thoughts. "So are you going with us, Nic?"

*What had they been talking about? Oh yeah. A trip somewhere.* "If I'm not on duty."

Rachel rolled her eyes. "Nic, it's this weekend. Remember? I have your schedule. I know when your four-days are. None of us want to go without you."

Ah, sweet. His ego was feeling better by the minute. Why was he letting a cool blonde and a toothless baby mess with his head?

Nic clapped his hands together. "Sounds good. You make the plans. I'll make the party."

Both girls laughed. Rachel tossed her hair over one shoulder. Nice hair. Nice girls. Fun times.

"You ladies up for a plate of my lasagna?"

Rachel touched her flat belly. "Can't. We're dieting. Swimsuit time."

"Don't know what you're missing." Slim Jim lifted his nearly empty plate above his recliner.

"Yes, we do," Mandy simpered. "Nic is a fabo cook."

"He'll make someone a great wife one of these days," Captain Summers added, his tone droll. "Did he tell you ladies about his new baby?"

Both women froze. Nic wished he'd had his camera phone ready to catch their shocked expressions.

"Get lost, Captain," he said mildly, and then to the girls. "He's kidding."

Yet, the mention of baby Alex started that strange yearning inside of him all over again.


Cassidy was a zombie.

"How's that design coming, Willis?" The art director of McMann's Marketing, Shane Tomlinson, was a go-getter, a type A personality who wanted everything done yesterday. On a normal day, Cassidy was right there with him.

But there was nothing normal about this week or the one that had preceded it.

"Fine," she muttered and reached for her coffee cup, hoping to appear cool and in control.

"Good. We need it ASAP." He tapped the top of her desk and wandered off to hassle another designer. Thank goodness.

For the past ten minutes, Cassidy had sat at her station staring mindlessly at the same rotating graphic. How was she supposed to create a new Web site for the Sports Emporium when all she could think about was sleep and Alex?

After four days and four of the longest nights of her life, she and her nephew had yet to establish a workable routine.

Workable? What a laugh. They had no routine at all. Alex cried and refused to sleep from dark to dawn. Cassidy rocked and sang and prayed and wondered if she'd lost her mind to think she could raise a child and keep her high-pressure career in fourth gear.

To make matters worse, after taking a week off, she was far behind. And today was the first day Alex had attended day care.

She glanced at the clock on her computer, then reached for her cell phone. She had the number on speed dial.

"Bo-peep Daycare," a chipper voice answered.

"This is Cassidy Willis. I'm calling to check on Alex Brown."

There was a slight pause. "Miss Willis, didn't you call about fifteen minutes ago?"

A lot could happen in fifteen minutes. "Is he all right?"

"He's asleep."

"That's what you said the last time."

"Babies generally nap for a couple of hours at a time."

Not at her place, he didn't. "Are you sure he's okay?"

"Positive."

"Will you check? I mean, right now. Go stand over his crib and look at him. Make sure he's breathing."

The day-care worker emitted a taxed sigh. "Stop worrying, ma'am. We take excellent care of our children."

That's what they all said. Yet, she'd seen the news reports, the horrors of day-care abuse. Bad things happened in some of them. How was she to know if Bo-peep was a good one or a bad one? Yes, she'd checked references, toured the facility, talked to other moms, but still…

"Please. Put the phone up to Alex's ear so he can hear my voice."

She didn't want him to feel abandoned.

"He's asleep. You don't want me to wake him, do you?"

"No, of course not." Yet she wondered at the woman's reticence. Was she hiding something? "Are you sure he's all right?"

Again that pause, only this time when the woman spoke, she was defensive. "Miss Willis, Alex is doing fine, but if you are that concerned, I suggest you come to the facility and have a look for yourself."

With a stammered thank-you, Cassidy snapped her flip phone shut and stared into space, deep in thought. After a couple of minutes, she dragged her purse out of the bottom drawer and jumped up. On her way out she passed Shane Tomlinson's office. She called, "Something important came up. I'll be back in twenty minutes."

Before her surprised boss could ask about the new Web design or remind her that she was days behind in work, she rushed out the door and down the elevator.

At ten o'clock that night Cassidy sprawled on her couch eating a convenience-store burrito while Alex gurgled happily on his play mat. Classical music, Beethoven's *Für Elise*, tinkled from the music box as colored lights responded to Alex's movements.

She felt like a hammered banana while Alex was rested and ready to rock and roll.

He looked up at her and smiled.

That quick her spirits lifted. Stuffing the last bite of burrito into her mouth she slid onto the floor beside him. No matter how exhausted, frustrated or lacking in confidence she might be, one smile from that face and she was mush. Sometimes she stared into his precious, innocent eyes and saw her sister. With every look, every splashing bath, every time he caught her finger in his little fist, Cassidy fell more in love. Terrified, inadequate, but in sappy, sloppy love.

No wonder her sister had been so happy. But how had she juggled taking care of Alex with working on the B and B? How did she manage to appear fresh and rested when, at times, she must have been as frantic and exhausted as Cassidy?

The answers would forever remain a mystery. Perhaps birth mothers received some influx of hormone that kept them going.

A hormone Cassidy lacked.

Lying on her belly, she talked to Alex, played with him and then tried once more to get him down for the night.

Her head ached from lack of sleep. The tension in her shoulders was tight enough to snap. Her eyes burned.

She gathered a wide-awake Alex close to her chest and rocked him in the bentwood rocker.

"Come on, lamb, help Aunt Cassidy out. I'm so tired. I have to work tomorrow, you know. If I don't work, I won't be able to buy those cans of formula you're so wild about."

She rubbed his rounded belly with the flat of her hand. He seemed to like when she did that.

Her fingernails, she noticed, were looking rough, but when would she have the time or energy to go to the nail spa? Her roots needed to be touched up, too. Hopefully, in another week Alex would be on schedule.

"Ready for sleepy-pie?" It sounded like a dumb thing to say, but lately Cassidy found herself saying all kinds of gibberish. What exactly *was* sleepy-pie?

With a shake of her head, Cassidy laughed at her giddy thoughts. At the same time Alex swung his hand, catching hold of her hair. Cassidy's head was yanked sideways. Tears smarted at the corners of her eyes. With painful care, she managed to peel back each tiny finger until she was free again. Alex laughed up at her.

"Come on, buddy. Please. Go to sleep. I'm going to lay you down in your crib like a big boy and turn on your favorite lullaby." She did so, simultaneously activating the video monitor over his bed.

He gooed happily, arms and legs waving. Slowly, breath held, she backed to the doorway. So far, so good. She snapped off the light. Only the tinkling lilt of Brahm's lullaby shimmered in the quiet.

With a relieved exhale, she tiptoed down the hallway and fell facedown, still fully dressed, on a down comforter that had cost three days' pay. Normally fussy about anything on top of that cover, right now she was too tired to care.

From the monitor at her bedside came the continuing sounds of lullabies and baby noises. All was well in the nursery. Maybe tonight was the night Alex would sleep.

Cassidy thought about getting up to read her devotional, something she hadn't done since Alex moved in. Instead, she muttered a half-baked prayer, eyes closed, body beginning to float away. Thank goodness. Rest.

The banshee cry shot a stinging bolus of adrenaline into her brain. She sat straight up.

"No. Please," she whimpered like a kicked pup. "Don't cry."

But the sounds from the monitor grew louder and more furious.

"What could he want?" He was fed, changed, warm. What could be wrong with him?

Cassidy brushed limp hair from her face and stumbled into the baby's room. "What is it, sweetheart? Tell Aunt Cassidy."

If only he *could* tell her. If only she understood his signals. Janna always said she could tell the difference between every cry.

"Not me." Every cry sounded the same—painful to the ears and nerves.

Maybe she didn't have the mother gene. "Lord, I'm trying. Show me what to do."

Such a pathetic prayer, she almost felt guilty for praying it.

"I want to make him happy. I want to be a good mom." She lifted Alex's stiff, screaming body against her shoulder. "I love you, Alexander Brown. I love you."

She began to swing her body back and forth, back and forth in what she hoped was a soothing rhythm. Alex kept crying.

Out on her feet, ready to collapse, she considered taking him into her bed. But if she lay down on the bed with him, she might fall asleep. Wasn't that a bad thing to do? Wouldn't she be in danger of rolling on him or something horrid like that?

Alex stiffened his whole body, pushing back from her shoulder to scream into her ear. His red, contorted face indicated something was wrong. But what?

She slid into the rocker again. What if she rocked herself to sleep and dropped him? The high-pitched crying rose a notch. Not much chance of falling asleep right now.

Arms heavy, head aching, she rocked and prayed. Alex found no comfort.

Her heart ached, too, knowing that Janna would have known what to do. Brad and Janna should be here, loving their baby, tending to his needs, not her. Not a workaholic aunt whose only venture into caregiving was a dozen exotic house plants.

She needed help. But who? Last night, she'd phoned every coworker she could think of. Some had laughed at her. Some had offered advice that hadn't worked. The trouble was, most of her friends were single.

"I know you miss your mommy, Alex." Tears pressed at the back of her eyelids. "I miss her, too."

Alex jerked his knees to his chest and screamed.

Cassidy paced to the front window, murmuring words of comfort and slips of prayers. Light from an apartment below and to the right of hers beamed like a beacon of hope.

James and Marla were still awake. Maybe they would have an idea.

Desperate, Cassidy muttered, "Any port in a storm."

The late April night was glorious. Usually, she would have sat out on the stairs and breathed in the scent of blooming lilacs and watched a handful of cars slide past. Not tonight.

In minutes she was pounding on the door of the apartment below. Loud barks greeted her as the door opened.

"Cassidy, hello." Marla was in her robe. The tiny woman of Thai heritage looked back over her shoulder toward the living area. "It's Cassidy, honey."

An indistinguishable male rumble answered.

Dismay drifted through Cassidy. She shouldn't have come. "Were you already in bed? Marla, I'm so sorry."

"No problem. We were watching *The Late Show*." She waved Cassidy inside. "What's going on?"

As if she couldn't tell, Alex lifted his face from Cassidy's shoulder, went momentarily silent while he took a long, searching look at Marla and then belted out another cry.

Two fat English bulldogs plopped onto their bottoms, heads cocked to one side in fascinated silence.

Marla's exotically beautiful eyes looked at Alex as if he were a Martian. "Why is he crying so hard?"

Cassidy's face crumpled in disappointment. "I was hoping you might know."

"Me? My babies are bulldogs, Cassidy, not humans."

"I know, but…" At a loss, Cassidy puffed out a sigh. "I guess I was desperate."

A tinkle of laughter erupted from Marla's lips. "To come to me, you surely were. I never even babysat."

"Me neither."

"Want me to hold him for a minute? You look like you're about to collapse."

"I am." Tears burned Cassidy's eyes as she handed him off. "I love the little guy. I'm just not a very good mother."

"Hey." Marla patted Cassidy's arm. "Give it some time. This is new for both of you."

"Maybe I should take him to the hospital," Cassidy said.

"Is he sick?" Marla's voice rose above Alex's crying.

"I don't think so. Anyway, he was all right when I picked him up at day care and they said he'd had a good day."

She didn't add that this was after she'd "dropped by" the place four times on unannounced visits. Every time he'd been asleep. She'd started to wonder if they drugged him. He certainly didn't sleep like that for her.

"Hmm. Well, I don't know. It seems pointless to take him to the emergency room for crying. What about a nice cup of chai?"

Cassidy's humor returned. "For me or Alex?"

Marla giggled. "Both of you. That's my solution anytime I'm upset. Chai, massage, pray." She held up a finger. "Good idea."

The tiny woman turned and yelled, a surprisingly loud noise coming from such a small body. "James, come in here. We need to pray with Cassidy."

Cassidy realized then that this was really why she'd come downstairs to the Taylor's place. James and Marla were the only other believers she knew in the apartment complex. The three of them, along with Janna and Brad, had shared a monthly cookout, Bible study and time of fellowship. She needed her neighbors even more now that Janna and Brad were gone.

James, a blond giant as opposite as could be in looks from his tiny, dark wife, padded barefoot into the living room wearing baggy shorts and a T-shirt. Both bulldogs jumped up, tags jingling, to greet him. He placed an enormous hand on one's head.

All this time, Alex continued to fuss, sometimes quietly, sometimes with earsplitting cries.

Marla, her face an amusing mix of horror and compassion, handed Alex off to her giant husband. Again, Alex stopped crying long enough to examine the new stranger. The two bulldogs sniffed at the baby's dangling feet.

"Let's pray while he's quiet," James said. Before Cassidy could get her eyes closed, he began. "Father God, Cassidy is new at this parent stuff. She needs some help. Guide her, give her wisdom."

"And some sleep," Marla said. "Every night."

"Yes, Lord," James picked up the tag-team prayer. "And help Alex adjust to his new situation and sleep like a baby, too. In Jesus' name."

All three said, "Amen."

"He isn't crying." Marla stroked a tiny, pink-nailed hand over the back of Alex's smooth, round head.

"Is he asleep?" Cassidy asked. Please say *yes*.

James leaned away from the baby and looked down. "No. Wide awake. One out of two isn't bad. At least he's quiet."

"For now," Cassidy said, taking him from the man's arms.

Though she hadn't accomplished anything as far as understanding Alex's problem, Cassidy felt better. James and Marla were unorthodox in some ways, but they had hearts for God.

"Thanks, guys." She turned to leave. "Go finish your show. I hope you haven't missed too much."

"We're good. TiVo," James said with a grin. Cassidy noticed the remote protruding from his T-shirt pocket. "This thing with Alex will work out. Don't worry."

Easy for him to say.

With a bulldog at either side, he opened the door and all

three faces—one large human and two fat canines—kept guard while Cassidy walked down the sidewalk and up the stairs to her apartment.

A siren split the night. Cassidy shivered and slammed the door, locking it. Someone somewhere was in danger.

Alex's fussing started up again.

So much for bothering the neighbors. But they had prayed, and with her fuzzy brain of late, her own prayers seemed to bounce off the ceiling. She only hoped God was listening and would show her what to do.

The sirens grew louder, reminding her of that tragic night and of Nic Carano.

She didn't want to think about it or about him. The fire had brought back terrible memories of the time she'd been alone and terrified, trapped under a mountain of rubble while the smell of death and distant smoke moved ever closer.

She shivered. For years, she'd tucked away the fear, but Janna's death had brought the memories back with a vengeance. Everyone she loved died tragically. Though in different ways, fire had been involved both times.

Fireman Nic was a reminder she didn't need.

But his family had brought her a baby book filled with advice. She'd been too busy and tired to read it.

The Caranos. Her exhausted mind drifted to Rosalie, the warm earth-mother woman whose babies probably had never cried. Like some sitcom mother of the fifties, Rosalie would have cradled one child, fed another, played with two others and baked a delicious Italian dinner for the family, all while running a bakery single-handedly and keeping a pristine house.

Nic's mother would know what to do with a baby who cried and refused to sleep at night.

A teensy bit of guilt nagged at her. Nic had phoned a few

times. She hadn't answered or returned his calls. He probably thought she was a snob. How could she explain that who he was and what he did for a living struck terror in her heart?

She couldn't, of course. Her fear was irrational.

Hopefully, Nic considered that she was busy adjusting to a baby in the house.

The notion almost brought a sob. Adjusting? No one was adjusting around here. Her work suffered. Her appearance suffered. Even her miniature lemon tree was droopy.

How had Rosalie Carano become a superwoman?

With Alex against her shoulder, she paced, trying to remember what she'd done with Nic's phone number.

When she found the slip of paper in the bottom of her purse, her shoulders sagged.

She had no right to call him. She didn't want to call him. But who else?

She battled her conscience. It was too late at night to call anyone. She'd already bothered the neighbors. And phoned her handful of good friends.

Alex shuddered against her, then wailed louder.

Was it incredibly rude of her to call a man she was trying to avoid?

More like incredibly desperate.

A guy like Nic would either be on duty at the fire station or out having fun. He would be awake. She could find out from him if it would be all right to call his mother.

Though aware that her brain was not working on all cylinders, Cassidy dialed anyway.

The line *brrred* in her ear. Twice. Three times. Cassidy bit her lip. What if she got his voice mail? What would she say? "Nic, I need your mother. Alex won't go to sleep, and I'm about to die over here?"

Pathetic. A stupid idea.

She must have been delirious to even consider calling Nic Carano.

Ready to hang up, she was lowering the receiver when a *snick* sounded.

A slightly slurred voice, deep and grumbly, muttered, "Party Central."

# Chapter Five

Nic pushed back the blanket and sat up, pressing the receiver to his ear. What was that racket? After the trip to Galveston, he had been dead asleep and had considered not answering the phone at all. Now he was glad he had. Someone was in trouble.

"Who is this? What's going on over there? Do I need to call 9-1-1?"

He swung his feet over the side of the twin bed—the same twin bed he'd slept in since he was twelve. His high-school baseball trophies still lined a shelf in the corner.

*Sheesh,* he thought. *Nic, when are you going to grow up, man, and break out of here?*

"Nic, I need your help."

The voice sounded familiar. Fumbling with the lamp at his bedside, he clicked on a light and squinted at the caller ID.

"Cassidy?"

"I'm sorry to call this late. You're probably busy."

Busy? His blurry eyes found the clock. Yeah, he was busy. Catching Zs. "Not busy at all. Just got back from the beach. What's going on over there?"

*And why are you calling me?* Not that he was complaining about hearing from her, but the timing was weird. Real weird.

"Alex won't stop crying."

Nic's ego whimpered. No woman had ever called to tell him about a crying baby. "Give him a bottle, maybe?"

"I did. I changed him. I rocked him, I walked him. I'm dying, Nic." The desperation in her voice was apparent. "I haven't slept in a week because Alex cries all night. I don't know what to do anymore."

Nic had visions of the breathy, gushing phone call he'd dreamed of getting from the sleek blonde. This was not it.

He got up and stumbled around his bedroom, kicking a lump of clothes out of the way, rubbing his chest as he shook off the cobwebs of sleep.

Certain he was missing something in this conversation, he asked, "Want me to come over?"

"No!"

"You said that too fast. Broke my heart right in half."

"Nic. This isn't funny. Is your mother up? I thought she might be able to give me some advice, but I didn't want to wake her."

She hadn't minded waking him though. Hmm. Interesting.

Suddenly wide-awake and feeling zippy, Nic said, "I'll be there in ten minutes."

"No, Nic. Your mom—" but before she could finish, he laughed softly and disconnected.

The woman intrigued him. And he was a sucker for Alex. Why not be a good little fireman and rush to the rescue?


Timing himself, Nic arrived at Cassidy's apartment in eight minutes. He could hear the little dude through the door. *Man, oh man*, he thought. No wonder Cassidy was on the verge of hysteria. The noise increased when she let him inside.

Without giving the motion any consideration, he took the baby from Cassidy's arms. "You look beat."

"I am."

She must be really tired. Most women of his acquaintance would be offended at such a comment.

The half-moons below Cassidy's eyes were dark and hollow, more so since the last time he'd seen her. Her eyes were bloodshot, her hair limp and disheveled.

He had the uncomfortable thought that she was pretty anyway. He must be as tired as she was.

"What's the matter with the little dude?" he asked, patting the baby's stiff back, the blue onesie pajamas soft beneath his fingers.

"I have no idea. That's why I wanted your mother."

"Mom would know." He led the way into the nursery and laid the red-faced, bawling baby on the changing table. "Maybe Uncle Nicky knows, too."

He wasn't a paramedic-turned-med-school wannabe for nothing.

"What?" She sounded on the edge—on the edge and leaning over the railing ready to jump.

Alex kicked and thrashed, inconsolable as Nic ran a gentle hand over his rigid tummy. "Feel how firm his belly is. Maybe he has a tummy ache."

Cassidy came up beside him, her side warm against his. She smelled like orange blossoms. Sweet. Very sweet.

Normally when Nic noticed a girl's cologne, he paid her a compliment. Not tonight. Though his nose couldn't help enjoying her scent, his focus was baby Alex.

"What do we do for him?"

"Not sure. Comfort him as much as we can until he gets over the worst of it, maybe?"

"Should I take him to the hospital?" she asked over Alex's intermittent outbursts.

Nic gazed down at the infant. "For a tummy ache? Nah, I don't think so. Seems like I remember my sisters talking about colic. Could he have colic?"

"You're asking me?" Her voice rose an octave. She looked frantic enough to cry. Nic couldn't stand for a woman to cry.

Digging hard into the recesses of his mind, he dragged up conversations between his sisters and mother. Baby and kid stuff came up a lot at his house, though he hadn't paid all that much attention. Still, with that many kids some of the info was bound to have stuck.

"If he has colic, I don't think there's much you can do."

"What's caused it? Did I do something wrong?"

"I remember my sisters discussing diet changes."

Nic stroked the squirming infant with one hand as Cassidy gazed up at him. Blue. Her eyes were the prettiest shade of blue.

"Alex certainly has had those," she said. "And a lot of other changes. Poor lamb. I feel so bad for him. He's stuck with an aunt who doesn't have a clue."

Nic blinked and dragged his gaze from Cassidy's blue, blue eyes to Alex. "Tell you what."

"What?"

"You get some sleep. I'll look after Alex."

Cassidy was already shaking her head. "I have to learn to cope. He's my responsibility."

She nudged him aside to check Alex's diaper, changed him, then lifted him against her shoulder. Nic didn't appreciate the brush-off. She'd called him over here. He wanted to do something.

So much for the trusty-firefighter-to-the-rescue scenario he'd imagined. This woman was messing up his knight-in-shining-turnout-gear fantasy.

"Does he cry like this every night?" He followed her into the living room, wondering what he was doing in Cassidy's apartment at two in the morning and why he didn't just hit the road? She didn't want him here.

No, wait, she *did* want him here. She'd called him.

Yep, she was definitely messing with his head. And he was just stubborn enough to stick around and see what happened.

Besides, he felt sorry for the little dude.

"He cries off and on every night from bedtime until morning. Then he sleeps like a rock at day care." Cassidy gnawed a pretty lip with white, even teeth. Some orthodontist had made a mint off Grandma Cruella. "Anyway, the day-care workers say he sleeps all day. I don't trust them."

"Why not?"

"How can he sleep all day when he's awake or crying all night?"

"There's your answer. He's tired. He has his days and nights confused."

"Oh." Drooping with fatigue, she sagged into a chair and propped Alex on her lap facing Nic. "Makes sense. But I still don't like putting him in day care. Janna never wanted that. She would be appalled."

Bad deal, but what choice did she have? "Necessary evil, I guess, for a single parent."

"I guess."

Cassidy's whole body was a study in exhaustion. Nic couldn't take it. Sure, he was a tad weary from three days of fun in the sun, but erratic hours had never bothered him. They were part of a firefighter's routine. On for twenty-four hours, off for a day, on again, and off for more days. A crazy life that fit him to a tee.

He reached for Alex and plopped down with him on the small couch, propping his feet on the ottoman. If she was too stubborn to get some sleep, at least he could give her some respite from Alex. The baby couldn't help having a bellyache and being confused with all the changes in his life.

With Alex over his shoulder, he patted and talked, the way he had done with his gaggle of nieces and nephews. Uncle Nic had been the favored babysitter. Well, maybe not by his siblings, but definitely by the kids. Even when they were infants like Alex, he'd enjoyed them, knowing when the going got rough, he could hand them back to their mothers.

He made up silly songs in the baby's ear, singing low and soft as he patted. Cassidy looked at him from beneath drooping eyelids and smiled. "That one didn't rhyme."

"What are you talking about? I won a third grade poetry contest. I am a master at the rhyming couplet. Convertible and Corvette in the same poem would make the Bard green with envy."

She laughed softly. A pretty sound. Had he heard her laugh before? If he had, he must not have been paying close attention.

He was paying attention now.

The last thing Cassidy remembered was thinking how cute Nic was and how delirious she must be to allow a firefighter—especially this one—in her apartment.

Slowly returning to consciousness, she adjusted the angle of her neck. A crick was in the making. She'd fallen asleep sitting up in a chair, listening to Nic Carano sing to Alex.

Nic Carano. Oh my goodness.

Her eyes popped open.

The darkly handsome firefighter no longer occupied the couch across from her. She glanced around the dimly lit room. Someone had turned off all the lights except for a small reading lamp.

"Nic?" she whispered. "Nic?"

Fear stood her on her feet. Nic was gone. So was Alex.

Hurrying now, she rushed into the nursery and nearly collapsed with relief. The baby lay in a hump, knees drawn up and tiny backside in the air, a blanket covering him. His back rose and fell in restful slumber.

Tiptoeing, afraid of waking him, she went through the apartment to check the door locks and then to make sure the smoke detectors were functioning. Finding all secure, she looked out into the parking lot. Nic's truck was gone. A car slid past on the street below, its lights washing the concrete in pale yellow before disappearing.

According to the artsy clock above her sofa Cassidy had slept several hours. Her alarm would go off soon.

Amazing. How had she slept so soundly while sitting up in a chair? She hadn't even heard Nic leave.

Heading toward the shower, Cassidy rubbed both hands over her groggy face.

She'd fallen asleep with a man in her apartment—a playboy firefighter, of all people—and Alex in pain. What kind of mother was she?

Guilt-ridden, Cassidy spent too much of the following workday telephoning the day care and researching four-month-old babies on the Internet. Then she made a long list of parenting dos and don'ts and scheduled an appointment with a pediatrician. Even though Alex had been thoroughly examined before dismissal from the hospital, Cassidy figured another exam was in order. This time she knew what questions to ask.

On her lunch break, which she had never taken before the baby came into her life, she drove to Bo-peep day care and played with Alex.

Her boss frowned when she walked in after an hour's

absence. "I need those mock-ups today, Cassidy. We have a production meeting with Carters at two and the design team meets after that."

"Right." She was a perfectionist in her job. Shane knew that. "I'll get it done." Somehow.

While Nic was comforting Alex last night, she should have whipped out the laptop and gotten busy on this project. But what had she done? She'd fallen asleep.

Since the fire, her creativity had gone flat. She was going through the motions, plugging in clichéd ideas that would get her nowhere. The company expected original, top-notch work from her. They'd always gotten it.

By the time the workday ended, she'd managed to throw together a couple of ideas, which she e-mailed to Shane's in-box. Her eyes burned and her neck ached. Four hours of sleep had been better than none, but she was still fatigued to the point of dropping. She wished for the time and energy to go for a run.

After picking up the baby and stopping by the supermarket for diapers, formula and a few groceries, she realized her running days might be over. She couldn't run and leave Alex alone in the apartment—even if she had the energy.

As she trudged up the stairs, baby in one arm, plastic grocery sacks dangling from her elbow and diaper bag and purse over the opposite shoulder, reality struck. Being a good mother was the hardest, most unselfish job on the planet.

And she had a lot of adjustments to make.

"You're worth it, though, my lamb," she said to the boy balanced between the crook of her elbow and her hip. She was determined to read and study and do everything in her power to become the best possible mother to this child who held her heart. No matter how much he cried, no matter how much sleep she lost, there were those special moments when he smiled or laughed and cooed up at her with recognition and pleasure. Then her heart filled with profound joy and the belief that together they would be a family. Somehow. If she could get it right and keep her job in the process. She owed that much to him and to Janna.

"Aunt Cassidy will do better, sweetie, I promise." She shifted him higher, balancing while she fumbled with the key.

An amused voice jolted her. "Talking to yourself?"

Cassidy jumped and dropped the keys.

Arms and ankles crossed, Nic Carano leaned against the railing outside her door. He wore a crisp, maize-colored shirt unbuttoned over a navy blue T-shirt that said, "Certified Hokey Pokey Instructor."

Cassidy ignored the sudden butterflies in her stomach. Nic looked as neat and fresh as a catalog model. She felt like the bottom of a clothes hamper.

"You scared me."

With a charming grin and easy grace, he retrieved the keys and unlocked the door.

As she stumbled awkwardly past, lugging too much stuff, Nic snatched the baby, swinging him high overhead. "Hey, Alex. How's my man?"

Alex gurgled happily, toothless mouth wide open. The sight was precious, endearing, and Cassidy's heart turned over with profound love for her sister's child.

"Be careful," she said. "He'll spit up in your face."

Nic's shoulders bunched. He grimaced and slowly returned Alex to a level position. "Was that the voice of experience?"

"Unfortunately." Cassidy dipped her head in wry concession and dropped the load of bags in the doorway. Her place was a mess. Baby toys scattered here and there. Unfolded laundry piled on the table. This morning's coffee cup and Alex's dirty bottles cluttered the sink. Until last week, she'd been a perfectionist here as well as at work. Anyone with off-white furniture had better be neat. Today she was too tired to care. "Sorry the place is a disaster."

"It is?" Nic's honest bewilderment made her laugh.

"Does that mean your apartment is less than tidy?"

"Room. I don't have an apartment. My mom says I'm a pig, a throwback to Great-Uncle Dominic." Still holding Alex, he plopped down on the sofa in the same spot he'd occupied last night. Alex grabbed Nic's bottom lip and pulled.

"You still live with your parents?" Hadn't she figured him for the type?

"For now." Nic extracted his lip from Alex's grasp and handed the baby a rattle. "I'm looking around. Time to get out on my own."

No kidding. She shuddered at the very thought of still living in Grandmother's house.

But then, the Carano family wasn't anything like her grandmother.

"The apartment directly below this one is open." As soon as she spoke the words, Cassidy wished them back. What was she thinking? She didn't want Nic Carano for a neighbor. She didn't even want him here now.

"That a fact?"

"Well, ummm," she stammered. "It's probably rented by now."

He studied her for a few seconds. Then he grinned. The cleft in his chin drew her attention. "You trying to discourage me?"

"I don't know what you mean."

Nic kept staring, eyes dancing with amusement.

She tugged at the collar of her blouse, aware of the heat that crept up her neck. Certain the dratted blotches would pop up on her skin any minute, Cassidy turned away, busying herself with straightening the living room.

"Why *did* you come over today?" she asked. And why did

Notorious Nic have to be the firefighter who rescued her nephew? "I mean, there's really no need. I appreciate all you've done, coming to my aid last night, but—"

"Are you telling me to hit the road?"

Hands filled with baby toys, she paused, "No!" *Yes.*

"Good. You were about to hurt my delicate feelings." He grinned at the statement. A man with his self-confidence would never believe he wasn't wanted. "Probably of more importance to you than my tender ego is this. I bring good tidings and words of advice from my mom, the baby expert."

All thoughts of getting rid of Nic fled. Cassidy stacked the colorful toys into an empty clothes basket and shoved it against the wall.

"What did she say?"

Nic dangled a set of plastic keys in front of the baby. "According to Mom, Alex has a big adjustment to make. Because of the new formula, he probably *is* having some colic like we thought last night, but the bigger issue is he's missing the familiar. He may only be a few months old, but he knew his mother and father. Now, when he's tired and nighttime comes, he looks for them. He wants them."

An ache of sorrow, never far away, surged inside Cassidy. She missed them, too. She wanted them, too. How much more, then, would a tiny baby long for his mother and father?

She slid onto the sofa to stroke Alex's hair. "She's right. He does. I hadn't realized it but he checks out every new face as if hoping to find Janna or Brad."

Both adults gazed at Alex. Nic spoke. "Sad deal."

Her heart heavy, Cassidy murmured softly, "I can never replace them."

"Don't beat yourself up. You're doing the best you can in a tragic situation. Mom says for you to just keep keeping on. In time he'll bond firmly to you and everything will be great."

In time. She didn't have time. Her job was floundering. Her body was a wreck. Beyond her work and Alex's care, she had the issues of Janna's estate to deal with. Talking to Grandmother made things worse, not better. She had no time.

More than anything she wanted Alex to be a happy, healthy, well-adjusted child. She prayed that she had what it took to give him that. God would not have put her in this position if she couldn't handle it. Would He?

Nic's cell phone played the "Looney Toons" theme. Nic whipped the phone from his pocket and held the music out for Alex's reaction before speaking into the mouthpiece. "Party Central."

Immediately Cassidy was aware that a female was on the other end. She tensed.

For some inexplicable reason listening to Nic chat up a girl-friend in her apartment made Cassidy uncomfortable.

She got up from the sofa, went into the kitchen and began slamming cabinets and rattling dishes. There was so much to do. Besides, she had no desire to hear Nic flirt with one of his girls. Really. He was exactly as she remembered—an ir-responsible charmer. Not that she cared. Not that she was interested.

She was simply grateful for his help. Last night, she'd been out of her mind to call him. Now, she'd have to be rude to get rid of him. But she couldn't do that. He and his family had been godsends—literally sent by God to help her and Alex in their time of need.

So now what was she supposed to do?

Wrinkling her nose at the sour smell, she dumped clabbered formula from a bottle she'd found in the bottom of the diaper bag and added the nurser to the others in the dishwasher.

An arm snaked around from behind her and added yet another bottle to the dishwasher. Cassidy jumped. She hadn't heard his approach. "Will you stop sneaking up on me?" *And will you stop forcing me to think about you?*

Standing a tad too close, he grinned, unrepentant. "You smell good."

She made a face, but her pulse tripped. "If you're fond of baby puke."

Nic laughed. He had a great laugh. "Look, I gotta go."

No surprise there. His entourage had called.

"But first, I have an idea."

"This came from your conversation with—what was her name?—Brittany?"

Drying her hands on a paper towel, she glanced around him, past the table and chairs into the open living area. Alex rested in his swing, grabbing happily at the overhead circus animals, the swing tick-tocking to the tune of "The Greatest Show on Earth."

"Brittany's a pal. We hang out."

A pal? Uh-huh. Bet Brittany didn't think that way. "So what's your idea?"

"I'm on duty tomorrow."

Cassidy stiffened at the reminder. Fire. Death.

"Can't come over."

Cassidy fluttered a hand against her chest. "You're breaking my heart."

Nic's lips twitched. "Smart mouth. We're talking about the little dude here. He's wild about me. What will he think if Uncle Nic doesn't stop by?"

"Modest," she said, rolling her eyes. But Nic was right. Alex lit up and hushed up when Nic played with him. "Don't worry about it. Now that I know what's wrong, I can handle everything."

Nic's voice gentled. "We all need a little help now and then, Cassidy." He touched her arm. Cassidy stepped back, breaking contact. If Nic noticed, he didn't react. "So what I'm thinking is this. The folks are having a cookout Sunday after church. You're invited. I'll pick you up about one o'clock. Baby advice from renowned Carano experts will flow. Many hands will hold and play with him, giving you a break. What do you say?"

What she wanted to say was "No way, get out, I don't understand why I'm letting you in my house." What she actually said was much nicer. "Life is crazy right now, Nic. I don't think so."

"All the more reason to come." He started toward the door, stopping to hand Alex a rattle before moving on.

"Thanks, Nic, but I can't."

He opened the door, then turned and pointed. "Think about it. I'll call you."

His footsteps echoed down the stairwell. Cassidy closed the door and looked at the baby happily babbling to a plastic lion. "Did Notorious Nic just ask me out?"

## Chapter Six

A curl of smoke snaked beneath the rubble of wood and brick where the ten-year-old lay trapped beneath a demolished school building. Cassidy could see the terrified, dirt-covered girl. Poor baby, she thought, and then with horror realized the child was her.

Her pulse jackhammered.

Somehow it had happened again. The earthquake had come back for her.

She struggled, fighting the rubble. Not again. Not again. "Mama! Daddy!"

The acrid smell of smoke crept closer. Fire was coming. She couldn't see it but it was coming. And she couldn't escape.

Something above her shifted. She tried to look up, but all was dark. The building trembled. Cassidy tensed, praying that nothing else struck her. She was thirsty. Her head pounded like the distant hammering.

Her legs and back ached, too, from the weight holding her captive beneath the school building—or what was left of it. Where were her friends? Where was her teacher? Where were Mama and Daddy? Why didn't they come?

"Somebody, please," she whimpered. Dust and ash flowed into her mouth.

Then the fire was upon her with its monster roar, licking at her face and hands. She was hot, burning.

She screamed…and bolted upright in bed.

For a second she didn't know where she was. She blinked into the darkness. All was quiet. No fire. No hammering. No painful press of rubble. Only the silky slide of sheets against her legs.

Realization flowed in and with it relief, sweet enough to taste. She was safe. She was an adult, not a helpless child, alone and trapped beneath a crumbling school.

Shaking all over and drenched in sweat, Cassidy rubbed both hands down her face. Her heart thudded loudly in the silence.

"A nightmare," she whispered into the darkness. The earthquake hadn't returned. She'd been dreaming again as she hadn't done in years.

Somewhere nearby, a siren wailed, a haunting cry of despair.

Cassidy kicked back the sheet that had wadded and tangled around her legs and went to the window of her second-floor apartment. The sirens must have awakened her. Either that or they'd invaded her subconscious and set off the dream.

She blew out a long, shuddering breath.

Nic Carano was on duty tonight. He was out there somewhere, facing the beast, facing death. She didn't want to worry about him, but she did. He'd saved Alex. He'd tried to save Janna.

Grief washed through her at the thought of her beloved sister, gone forever. She sagged against the window.

Though the night was warm, the smooth wood beneath her feet was as cold as her insides. With a shiver, she wrapped her arms around her waist and stared out into the dark night. Streetlights cast eerie shadows onto the parking lot below. No one stirred in this residential neighborhood.

Another siren added to the mournful cry.

Someone in this pleasant, upscale city had awakened to a living nightmare. Nic was out there with them.

"Father in Heaven," she whispered against the cool window-pane. "Don't let anyone die tonight. Surround them with your protection. Just as you protected the children of Israel from the fiery furnace, protect Nic and his crew and the people they're trying to help."

Yet the prayer didn't stop the quaking in her middle.

A week ago she wouldn't have given Nic Carano a thought. Regardless of her resistance, he'd charmed his way into her life. He'd been kind to Alex. Now he could die. In the short time they'd been reacquainted, she'd already heard stories about his antics. Nic Carano was not a cautious man.

She put a hand to her throat. This was why she couldn't let Nic come any nearer. This was why she'd refused his invitation. The danger was too great.

Trying to shake off the morbid thoughts, Cassidy padded into the nursery. The glow of the angel night-light illuminated Alex's round, cherubic face. Fist against his bow-shaped mouth, he stirred and made sucking noises but didn't awaken with his usual howl. For once, the baby slept soundly. It was the aunt who couldn't rest.

Reassured that Alex was safe, Cassidy moved from room to room checking each smoke detector. Satisfied that all were activated, she returned to bed.

In the dark silence, Cassidy willed her heartbeat to slow, willed her mind to stop circling around the nightmare and prayed for Alex's rescuer.

Sleep didn't come for the longest time.

Cassidy had thought about the nightmare—and Nic—all the next day and finally satisfied her concerns that evening by phoning Rosalie Carano. Nic was fine, as she'd known he would be, and then she'd felt a little silly for calling. True to her nature, Nic's mother had been warm and wonderful, a fact that made Cassidy acutely aware that she'd rarely had a mother to turn to in times of need. It also made her aware that there was more to Nic than he let on.

She and Rosalie had ended up talking about the Lord and babies and finally about Nic. Cassidy hadn't wanted to hear charming stories about the firefighter, but courtesy bade her listen.

As if that wasn't bad enough, by the time Sunday rolled around, the troublesome firefighter had telephoned twice and appeared on her doorstep another two times. He was becoming a pest. An attractive pest, yes, but an uncomfortable one, as well.

What did the man want anyway? Certainly not her. He had a host of women at his beck and call. Besides, if she was in the market for a man—which she wasn't—Nic could not be the one. He had two strikes against him. He was Notorious Nic with a girl for every day of the week, and more importantly, his job gave her nightmares. She would never, ever date a man who risked death every time he went to work.

Alex the traitor, however, went into ecstatic gyrations at the sound of Nic's voice. The baby was too young to associate the man with the event that had changed his life forever. Unfortunately for Cassidy, she remembered all too clearly.

Yet, Nic still came over. He still called. And the bond between him and Alex grew exponentially.

"We're not going to the cookout, Alex, and that's all there is to it," she said to the baby cradled in her arms. Muddy blue-brown eyes gazed earnestly back at her as his greedy mouth pulled on a bottle of formula.

"No use making a fuss," she went on. "Like half the female

population of Northwood, you are enamored of Nic's charm. You simply don't understand the problems the way I do."

And understand she did. Nic brought back too many memories, too much pain. Being around him had uncovered the shallow grave of buried trauma. Twice more this week she'd had nightmares. Though these were a combination of the earthquake that had stolen her parents and the fire that killed Janna, they were both vivid and terrifying. The residual effects lingered for hours afterward, stealing any hope of sleep.

Cassidy squeezed her eyes tight against the visions. She was so tired, like a minnow swimming upstream against a flood.

That morning in church she'd experienced a few minutes of peace and comfort. People were kind, thoughtful, interested in the tragedy that had made her Alex's guardian, but once outside the church doors, Cassidy felt alone again. She was certain the feeling was magnified by the unrelenting fatigue.

If only she had time to lie down and take a long, long nap. Three weeks' worth.

Alex waved his chubby arms as if to remind her that he was with her. A bubble of love replaced her melancholy thoughts.

Without Alex she might have sunk into despair and never come out again.

"I love you." Cassidy leaned forward to kiss the slobbery face, an action she'd have considered a little disgusting a few short weeks ago. Now, everything about Alex struck her as precious and beautiful. In unexpected moments like this, a kind of love she couldn't explain flooded over her in sweet waves.

The telephone jangled. Holding Alex in one arm with the bottle stuck under her chin, she answered the phone with the opposite hand. "Hello."

"Cassidy. This is Grandmother."

Cassidy's shoulders tensed. "How are you, Grandmother?"

"The question, dear, is how are you?"

"Coping."

The nasal voice pounded at her. "Exhausted? Frustrated? Realizing that raising a child is not an easy task?"

All that and more, but she was not about to admit as much to Grandmother.

"We're getting along great," she said with false cheer. "Alex is a wonderful baby."

A moment of silence hummed between them. Cassidy remained quiet, determined not to let her grandmother know how difficult things had been.

"I know of a good family here in Dallas that would be willing to take him." Eleanor's tone was crisp and business-like, as though she was selling real estate.

Cassidy's jaw tightened against the wash of pain. Had Grandmother ever loved anyone? "We've discussed this. Alex stays with me permanently. The subject is closed."

"Don't let sentimentality ruin your career."

Sentimentality?

Cassidy felt the soft roundness of Alex's body cradled against her, felt the movement of his little feet against her side, heard the sweet murmurings he made whenever she fed him. She glanced down into his beautiful face, aching with a love she couldn't explain to anyone, much less Eleanor Bassett. Grandmother had no clue what she was missing.

Cassidy knew if she didn't get off the line now, she'd say something regrettable.

Holding the phone tight enough to whiten her knuckles, she said, "If you'll excuse me, Grandmother, Alex and I have an outing planned. Thank you for your concern."

Without giving Eleanor a chance to reply, she replaced the receiver. It was only then that she realized Alex's great-grandmother had not even asked about him.

Heart heavy, though she should have expected this from

Eleanor Bassett, Cassidy finished feeding Alex and then changed him.

Grandmother's words were a reminder that her career was indeed going down the tubes. Friday, she'd missed another half day's work to take Alex to the pediatrician. Her boss had rejected the designs she'd submitted, asking for new ones by tomorrow. In addition, the advertising firm needed several other logos and brochures for which she was primarily responsible, and she'd missed a meeting with a key client. To move up the ladder, she had to perform, and this week, for the first time in her career, she'd been reprimanded by her superior for poor performance.

Her head hurt from trying to be a good mother while also trying to be more creative in her work. Women who did it all were superheroes.

Someone pounded on the door and a male voice called, "Open up. Your ice cream is melting."

And if she didn't already have enough problems to solve, there was Nic Carano.

Braced to remind him that she had, indeed, refused to attend his family's cook-out, Cassidy opened the door.

Nic, in a black T-shirt inscribed with "First things first, but not necessarily in that order," held a pink ice-cream cone in each hand. His maize-striped overshirt was unbuttoned as usual. Black hair shining in the sun, he looked good. Real good.

Ah, the beauty of Italian heritage. It should be outlawed.

Alex surged forward, nearly wrenching himself out of Cassidy's arms. She grappled to hang on.

Nic grinned, teeth white against his olive skin. "Trade you."

Ignoring the unwanted flare of attraction, Cassidy took one of the cones and slid Alex into the firefighter's hold. "How did you know to buy strawberry?"

"A guess. You don't look like the chocolate type."

She turned and started inside, feeling him there behind her.

"I could be vanilla," she shot over one shoulder.

"Oh, no." He shook his head as he followed her into the living room. "No one could mistake you for plain vanilla."

She spun around, cone pointed at him. "Is that a compliment?"

His eyes twinkled below one quirked eyebrow. "Maybe."

*Okay, enough already, Cassidy,* she thought. *No flirting allowed, no matter how charming and cute and hunky he might be.*

As a distraction, she tasted the soft ice cream. The cool burst of strawberry tantalized her tongue.

Cassidy rounded the back of the off-white couch, stopping there to lean. Having furniture between her and Nic might be a good idea, especially considering how her skin tingled and her pulse jumped around like frogs on a sidewalk.

"I thought you were going to a cookout," she said.

"I am." Balancing Alex easily in one arm, Nic took a giant lick of his double dip. "Good stuff, huh?"

"Great stuff. Thank you. But won't ice cream ruin your appetite?"

"Never put off the good things in life. Dessert first. Burgers later."

Making himself at home at one end of the couch, Nic crossed an ankle over one knee. Then he propped the baby in the resulting valley. Alex bicycled his arms, as if trying to reach the ice-cream cone.

"Think it's okay if Alex has a bite of this?"

He was asking her? "I don't know. Should babies have ice cream?"

Nic's shoulders lifted. "It's milk."

"True."

Though she had reservations, about both the ice cream and the man, Cassidy gave up the battle and settled on the opposite end of the couch to watch as Nic dabbed a bit of strawberry ice cream on Alex's tongue. The baby's face contorted, his tongue worked in and out. Pink melted ice cream slid down his chin.

Nic laughed, a rich sound that warmed a cold place inside Cassidy. The reaction startled her. She didn't want to *see* Nic, much less be attracted to him.

She whipped a wet wipe from a box on the end table and caught the drip before Alex's clean shirt could be soiled. The action put her shoulder to shoulder with Nic, the top of her head resting just below his chin. She could hear him breathe and smell the scent of warm cologne mingled with cold strawberry ice cream.

*Oh dear.*

Abruptly, she moved away.

Nic noticed. Contemplative eyes the color of French roast coffee watched her.

Cassidy's pulse stuttered. Her breath stuck in her windpipe. She dropped her gaze, wanting to reclaim Alex and run away, though there was no escaping her jumbled emotions.

After another uncomfortable second in which Cassidy searched for something clever to say, Nic crunched the edge of his waffle cone and raised an eyebrow. "Ready to head over to my place?"

Not on your life, buddy.

Drawing upon the cool demeanor that had won her the title of "ice queen" in college, Cassidy shook her head. "Can't. I'm sorry. When you knocked I was getting ready to put Alex down for what I hope is a long nap so I can work."

Nic paused on his way to another bite of waffle cone. "Work? On what?"

"Designs for a major client. I've fallen behind." She didn't add the rest. If she didn't catch up, her chances for promotion to creative director this year would be down the tubes.

"You're turning down an afternoon of fun with a terrific guy like me in favor of work?" His expression was comical. "This is painful."

"Call Brittany. Or Rachel." Both women had phoned more than once in her presence.

The comment had the opposite effect she'd intended. Nic seemed delighted.

"Are you jealous?" he asked, grinning like a maniac. "I'd feel a lot better if you'd say you are."

Not even close. The one thing she would not ever be was one of Nic's entourage. If he was the least bit interested in her, which he couldn't be, she would run in the other direction. Nevertheless, the notion that he might be made her more anxious than her own unacceptable attraction.

Keeping it light, she quipped, "Jealousy keeps me up at night."

"Oh, good. I thought Alex was doing that."

She made a face. "Funny."

"Yeah, I'm a funny guy. A barrel of laughs." For a minute, his relentless cheer faded.

Cassidy blinked at the change, wondering if there was a serious side to Notorious Nic. The idea made her more uncomfortable.

"Anything I can say to convince you to go to the cookout?" he asked after a minute. "You could use some R and R after the weeks of stress. And there's always that expert baby advice I promised." He placed a palm over the left side of his chest. "Along with mending my broken heart, of course."

He was kidding. He had to be kidding, but the man was charming to the max. Convincing, too. An afternoon of mindless relaxation sounded like a dream, but not with Nic Carano.

"I can't. Really, Nic. Thanks anyway."

"Another time maybe?"

Why was he so insistent?

She raked splayed fingers through the top of her hair. "Probably not."

"Okay. But you don't know what you're missing." He sighed, resting his chin on Alex's soft blond hair. "Mind if I take the little dude then? The folks were pretty taken with him."

So was Nic, which should eradicate any concerns she had about his interest in *her*. This was about Alex, the baby he'd bonded with during a tragedy.

Nic Carano was not interested in her as a woman. He had plenty of those.

Any twinge of disappointment on her part was purely wounded pride.

"I don't think that's a good idea." She didn't want her baby out of her sight, much less hanging out with a playboy fireman.

"Ah, come on. You'll have a chance to rest and work without interruption."

"A run," she said without thinking.

"Huh?"

"Since Alex came along, I've not had time to run."

"Great then. I'll take him. You run, rest, work, whatever."

"No!" How had she gotten into this? "Nic, I don't want to seem ungrateful, but I'm not ready to be away from Alex any more than I have to be. Understand?"

He tilted his head to one side, clearly *not* understanding. "No, but I respect your decision."

Without further argument, he handed the baby to her and headed for the door.

Feeling inexplicably guilty, she followed him. Was he angry? Upset? Hurt? "Thanks for the ice cream."

With a final wink and a quick salute, he pounded down the metal steps, open shirt flying in the breeze.

If she'd hurt his feelings, she was sorry. He'd been nothing but kind. At the same time she was relieved to have him gone.

Maybe he wouldn't come around anymore. Maybe she'd seen the last of Nic Carano.

She hadn't.

Tuesday morning as she dragged herself down the stairwell toward the parking lot, toting more than her body weight, she spotted a swarm of familiar dark heads on the sidewalk. She squinted through the overbright sunlight, shaking the cobwebs out of her sleep-deprived brain.

The Carano brothers? Surely not. Why would they be at her apartment complex at seven in the morning? Must be someone else.

In her foggy-headed condition, the newcomers could be the royal princes and she wouldn't recognize them. She needed coffee, but since Alex, those little extras had gone by the wayside. She'd barely gotten the two of them dressed, him fed, the diaper bag packed and her hair and makeup in place. She didn't dare arrive late to work another morning.

Suddenly, the man she did not want to think about came jogging up the steps looking poster-boy neat, his affable smile in place.

"You look grumpy," he said.

She glared at him. How dare he look happy and handsome at seven in the morning?

"I am. Go home."

With an annoying grin, he relieved her of all baggage except her purse and Alex. "I am home. Or I will be by noon."

Cassidy stopped dead, one foot on a step and one on the ground. A frisson of worry tingled up her spine. "What are you talking about?"

"The apartment you mentioned. I've finally made the break."

His words registered. Her heart tumbled to the concrete and lay there, shuddering. This couldn't be happening. The man she didn't want to be attracted to was now going to live too close to ignore.

"You rented the apartment below mine?" The words came out as flat as her mood.

Nic didn't notice. With his usual blithe spirit, he said, "Great, huh? Now I can pop up and see Alex any time. If you're really good, I might even babysit for you while you run."

That part sounded good. The rest, not so good.

Plodding on to her Camry, with Nic tagging along talking a mile a minute, the possibilities whirled inside Cassidy's head.

A firefighter living below her. The firefighter who was a walking, talking memory of one of the worst nights of her life. The firefighter who couldn't seem to take no for an answer.

*Lord,* she thought, the Bible says, *You'll not put more on me than I can stand. This is getting real close.*

Nic jogged ahead of her, too cheerful for anyone this early in the morning, and opened the back car door. Without saying a word, though she was reluctantly grateful for the extra hand, Cassidy strapped Alex into his car seat. When she turned to take the diaper bag and laptop from Nic, he had bounced around the car and was putting them on the other side.

"Thanks," she said grudgingly and got into the driver's seat.

Nic, all smiles and oozing charm, stood between her and the opened door, one elbow leaning on the upper edge. He bent toward her. He smelled good—like a recent shower and some subtle men's cologne. "What time do you get home?"

"Six," she answered, her mind occupied with noticing him more than she wanted to. "Why?"

"Lasagna. I'm great with lasagna."

He wanted to cook for her? "I might be running late. Work is backed up."

"No problem. Lasagna will wait."

"Oh, well…" What did she say to that?

"Hey, Nic," a male voice called. "Are you going to move this couch or romance the neighbor?"

Great. Everyone in the apartment complex probably heard that remark.

"Bye, Nic." Cassidy reached for the door handle. Her elbow bumped his side.

He stepped back and shot her a jaunty salute. Right before he shut the door, he said, "It's going to be great being neighbors."

*Great* was not the word Cassidy had in mind.

# Chapter Seven

"Come on, Nic. A trip to the lake won't be any fun without you."

Rachel drew her long brunette hair over one shoulder and looked at him with big, sad eyes. She and Mandy had dropped by with a pan of fresh chocolate brownies and a housewarming gift—a color-changing mood bowl.

"For chips and dip and conversation," the girls had said.

Whatever. He'd probably eat Cheerios out of it in the morning to find out what kind of mood he was in. Or maybe run the bowl upstairs and have Cassidy eat from it and check out her mood, which changed with the wind. She had been none too excited this morning to discover he was moving in below. What was with her anyway? One day she was begging him to come over and the next she wanted him out of her sight.

Challenging woman. No wonder he liked her.

"Nic, are you listening to me?" Mandy cocked her head, pouting a little. Her pout usually got to him. Not today.

"Sure I am." He grinned and reached for one of the brownies. "What did you say?"

She bopped him on the arm. Chocolate crumbs scattered on the floor. "You were a million miles away. What's going on with you?"

"Moving, I guess. Pretty busy around here." He stuffed the brownie into his mouth all at once and wiped his fingers down the legs of his jeans. Had he remembered to eat lunch?

"We came to help." Rachel motioned toward a stack of cardboard cartons lining the wall in the living room. "Show us where you want the things in these boxes and we'll put them up."

He waved them away. "Nah. I'm good. Thanks anyway." *And when are you leaving?* The last thought came out of nowhere. Normally, he liked having his friends hang out.

"If *we* put things up," Mandy said, poking through a box of linens his mother had donated. "He'll never find them."

"True." Rachel twisted the ends of her hair. "Guys have their own system."

"Yeah," Nic said, fingering the mood bowl. "Toss it in a drawer or under the bed."

"Nic!" Both girls laughed.

"Come on, Mandy." Rachel hiked a tiny silver purse over one shoulder. "Nic doesn't have time to play today. Let's go."

Nic was relieved. As much as he liked his friends, today he wanted some downtime. He had a million things on his mind and none of them was a trip to the lake or a party. Man, he must be having some kind of crisis.

He checked the mood bowl. It was still white, whatever that meant.

Setting the dish aside, he edged the girls toward the door as subtly as possible.

"Are you sure you won't go with us tomorrow?" Mandy asked when they were out on the sidewalk.

He didn't like to disappoint anyone, but he had things to do. Lately, he wasn't in the mood for their constant fun and games. He needed to study if he was going to pass his med school entrance exam next go-round, one of the main reasons for renting this apartment. Not that he would share that information with Rachel and Mandy. He had a reputation to uphold.

Most people, including his family, doubted he had what it took to get into medical school in the first place. If he failed again, they'd never know. If he passed, they'd finally see him as something besides a goof-off.

Maybe he needed to prove something to himself, as well.

"You'll have a great time," he told the girls. "Don't even think about me."

Resigned, the pair hopped into a yellow sports car and backed out, bracelet-bedecked arms waving out the windows.

With a relieved sigh, Nic started to close the door when he saw Cassidy's blue Camry pull up. All of a sudden, he was in the mood for company.

He jogged down the sidewalk to the parking lot, waited for her to kill the motor and then he opened the back door. The little dude was asleep, his head lolling to one side so that Nic felt sorry for him.

Cassidy pivoted around in the seat to stare. "Are you trying to kidnap my baby?"

"Rescuing. His neck is breaking." He unlatched the harness and gently lifted Alex into his arms, his attention on the series of straps holding the car seat in place. "I'll come back later and check your car seat. Did you have it professionally installed?"

Cassidy stepped out of the car and slammed the door. "No. This is the car seat your sister gave me."

"My bad. I should have installed it properly for you that day." He tapped his chest. "Certified baby seat installer."

She laughed.

He shot her a mock scowl, feeling zippier by the minute.

She looked pretty standing in the sunshine, her sleek blond hair catching the light. When she moved, a pair of big silver earrings danced around her face.

Even after a day's work and with bags under her eyes, Cassidy looked good to him. He was a little worried about that. He liked girls and thought every one of them was pretty, but Cassidy had started to stand out from the crowd. Before, all the girls were friends, pals, good times, but there was something different with this lady.

Nic looked forward to finding out exactly what that delectable difference *was*. Nothing serious, nothing heavy, but he was intrigued.

Alex woke up and turned sleepy eyes on him. He was fond of the little dude, too.

"Don't laugh," he said. "Firefighters take a course in this stuff. Safety first. I know my way around a baby seat."

"I learn something new every day." Cassidy pulled the diaper bag and laptop from the opposite side of the backseat. She was tired, as usual. He could see the fatigue hanging off her like weights. Strong lady, this one. A do-it-or-die-trying kind of woman. He liked that about her.

"Well, add this to your list." He followed Cassidy up the stairs where he took the key and opened the door.

She trudged inside and dumped the load on a red stuffed chair, the rare splash of color in the off-white room. "What?"

He handed Alex to her. "I'm going down to finish up dinner. The place is still a mess but the food will be awesome. I promise. You and my main man here spend some quality time, take a little rest, and then come on down."

"I should stay home and work."

He'd known she would argue and he was ready.

"You have to eat anyway." She was thin enough without skipping meals. "Come on, a relaxing, painless dinner, and then you can come back up here and work yourself into a coma. I'll even show you my mood bowl."

He'd meant the last crack to be funny. She didn't bite. "Why are you doing this?"

"I told you. I'm a great guy. Irresistible." He hoped she was buying this load of garbage. He wasn't sure why he needed to do things for her but he did. Maybe he felt responsible because he'd been there the night of the fire. Maybe the reason was a smiley-faced orphaned boy whose eyes sparkled as though Nic was the greatest thing since milk. Or maybe it was Cassidy herself. Whatever the reason, he wanted to find out.

"Did you get everything moved in this morning?"

"My brothers helped. We dragged everything inside. I'll need a few days to set up."

She kicked her shoes off and settled Alex on a play mat next to the red chair. A push of the button and classical music poured out with a tinny sound. Mozart, maybe, but what did he know of classical music, other than his dad's favorite operas?

"Didn't your friends help you unpack?" She gave Alex's back one last pat and straightened.

"Friends?"

Cool blue eyes scrutinized him. "The two girls who were leaving as I drove up?"

The question tickled him. "I love it when you get jealous."

One finely shaped eyebrow twitched. Man, she had pretty eyebrows.

"You wish."

Did he? Maybe. "Want me to take Alex down to my place while you grab a nap?"

She was shaking her head before he could finish. "Thanks but no."

He knew she'd say that. She didn't want Alex out of her

sight. "All right then. Come on down when you're ready. I have a present for you."

Surprised interest lit her expression. "A present? What is it?"

Nic grinned. A present was always good for persuading the reluctant. "You'll find out. See you in a few."

Cassidy plopped down on the couch for fifteen minutes with her feet up while she stewed about the problem of Nic Carano. Having him pop in or call had been bad enough, but now the guy was right downstairs and showed no signs of leaving her alone.

To make matters worse, she liked him. Somewhere beneath all that fun-and-games charm was a solid man, maybe a little off-center but dependable in the most surprising manner. She didn't much like thinking of him that way, but what else could she think? He'd been there when she needed him. Even with his reputation as a loose cannon, he'd saved Alex's life. How much more responsible could you get than that?

The thought depressed her. There was the main reason she couldn't let herself get too involved with Nic. Besides the females flitting around him like pretty painted butterflies, his career put him in danger every time he went on duty. She couldn't bear the thought of caring about someone else who might die tragically.

Yet, Nic was here, there, everywhere. What was she supposed to do about that?

Rubbing the ache in her temples, she came to a decision. There was nothing she could do about having Nic Carano as a neighbor. She couldn't very well have him evicted. So, she would simply block out any knowledge of his profession and be a good neighbor, a friend, but nothing more. As long as she kept an emotional distance, she was safe.

She hoped.

By the time she and Alex arrived at Nic's apartment nearly an hour later, Cassidy felt better, at least enough to look forward to eating a real meal for a change. There was something about having a man cook for her that inspired a surge of energy.

When he spotted Nic, Alex went into his usual ecstatic bounces and squeals. Cassidy, in spite of her good intentions, couldn't really blame him, though she kept her reaction under better control.

"The lasagna smells incredible," she said, nose tilted as she sniffed the air.

"Mama's special recipe." He waved them inside with a loaf of Italian bread. "She learned it from her mama who immigrated from Sicily after the war."

"Not many guys can make lasagna." Going down on one knee, Cassidy settled Alex on the carpet next to the couch. From there she could see him no matter where she was in the combination living/dining room.

"All five of us kids cut our teeth in the family bakery. A Carano who can't cook would have to change his last name."

"Where's my present?"

"Impatient woman." Shaking his head, he *tsk-tsked*. "Later, gator. If I give it to you now, you might run off."

With a smile acknowledging the humor, Cassidy quickly and, she hoped, surreptitiously surveyed the room in search of a smoke detector. The apartment layout was similar to hers, so escape routes would be the same. Reassured, Cassidy pushed up from Alex's side.

"I brought one for you." She offered Nic a small potted plant from her collection.

He looked at it as if it were the mystery meat in the school cafeteria. "What's this?"

"A plant, you goob."

"I figured out that part. I mean, why?"

"A housewarming gift. It will oxygenate your apartment."

"Oxygen is good." His head bobbed a couple of times. "Will you come over and water it for me?"

She ignored the question. "This is a Venus fly trap. His name is Michelangelo. He eats flies."

"No kidding? Real flies?" When she nodded, he considered the greenery with new respect. "Awesome. No sprays or swatters. And *zap*, dead fly. How sweet is that?"

"I thought a guy would appreciate the dead fly part." She took the plant away from him and glanced around for a place to set it. Boxes and clothes and a variety of odds and ends lay scattered about the place. Cassidy maneuvered around the biggest piles to plop Michelangelo in the middle of a very cluttered table. "Can I do something to help with dinner?"

"Everything is under control. Grab a glass of soda or whatever you want from the fridge and relax. Check out my mood bowl." He indicated an ordinary-looking white bowl on the counter. "Maybe you can tell me what to do with it."

"Mood bowl?" She studied the bowl, pretending to be serious. "Is it designed to determine mood or set the mood?"

"You got me. But I think it works. I've been in a good mood ever since you arrived."

Cassidy pulled a silly face, "Ha-ha. Cute."

Looking amazingly proficient in the kitchen, Nic responded with his usual cocky grin. Before she'd arrived, he'd tied a dish towel around his waist which did nothing to detract from his masculine good looks. Now, he slid a white quilted oven mitt onto one hand—a replica of the Arby's restaurant mascot, complete with a printed-on face. Cassidy smiled. Now that was the Nic she remembered.

Taking a can of diet soda from the fridge, she held up another. "Want one?"

"Sure. Not the diet stuff, though. I bought that for you."

She blinked. "How did you know?"

"I'm observant. You had a can in the cup holder of your car."

"Impressive."

He pulled a beautiful dish of lasagna from the oven. The smell of oregano and spices was strong enough to make Cassidy's stomach leap with excitement.

"I haven't had a home-cooked meal in—" she paused, not wanting to go there. Her last home-cooked meal had been made by Janna. "—a long time."

"You should have come to the cookout at my folks'. Lots of great homemade stuff."

Without being asked, she found the box containing dishes, took out a couple of place settings and scooted an array of odds and ends to one end of the table. Finding no napkins, she opted for paper towels, a roll of which lay on top of a box. Not exactly up to Grandmother's formal style, but pleasant and functional.

"Sit." Nic surprised her by politely pulling out a chair and waiting until she'd obeyed.

"Alex—" she started.

"Alex is fine where he is. I've got my eye on him. Stop worrying."

Sure enough, the baby lay on the blanket where she'd placed him, pushing up with his chubby arms to watch the adults with interest. From somewhere two colorful toys had appeared. Had Nic put those there?

"I could help get the food on the table." But her back ached from lugging Alex around, and it felt wonderful to sit and do nothing for a few minutes.

"Nope. You're my guest. I can't impress you if I don't do it all myself."

So she watched with interest as the ever-surprising Nic efficiently prepared dinner, casting frequent glances at Alex, and kept up a running conversation about her job, their mutual friends in college and his family.

"Tell me," Nic said as he sat down at her elbow—the only other clear spot on the table—and pushed the food in her direction. "Is Alex sleeping better at night? Or maybe I should ask if you're sleeping better?"

She took a hearty helping of the steaming lasagna. "A little. We're starting to adjust."

"I hear a 'but' in that sentence."

"It's hard, Nic," she admitted, aware of how easily she could talk to this man. "I never realized how much work being a mother is."

"You're also holding down a full-time job."

"True. But if I don't pick up pace at work I won't have a job at all, much less advance in my career."

"Is the problem serious?"

"Frighteningly so. I missed an important deadline with a client."

"Not the end of the world."

"It wouldn't be if other things weren't going wrong and falling behind."

"Anything I can do to help?"

What an interesting question. She shook her head. "I appreciate the offer, but I'm on my own."

Nic snagged a chunk of the fresh bread he'd brought from his family's bakery and slathered it with real butter. "Yeah, about that. Would I be prying to ask what happened to your parents?"

Over the years, she'd encountered the question dozens of times. She never let herself think deeper than the surface.

With little emotion, she swallowed a bite of cheesy lasagna and said, "They died when I was ten and Janna was seven."

"Wow, bad deal. So that's how you came to live with Cruella de Vil?"

"Nic," she tried to scold, but her lips quivered with humor. "Grandmother did her best. She just isn't that good with children."

"Or puppies." His eyes danced. "Sorry."

"No, you aren't."

"Well, no. I'm not. So, what happened? To your parents, I mean. Car accident?"

Cassidy fiddled with the salad on her plate. Most people let the topic drop when she did. Not Nic. He had to pry. "They were missionaries teaching in a Christian school in the Philippines. There was an earthquake. The building collapsed."

The buttery bread paused halfway to his lips. "Oh man. Cass."

The sympathy in his dark eyes got to her in a hurry. A trembling started way down in her bones, the flood tide of emotion rumbled like a threatening volcano.

Cassidy licked her suddenly dry lips. "I haven't talked about this in a long time."

No one knew of the terror she'd sublimated in childhood, scolded by her grandmother, called a baby for being afraid in the dark. Thank God Janna had been spared and had never really known what Cassidy had gone through. She'd been in the States, quarantined with chicken pox.

Nic chewed and swallowed. "You don't have to tell me if you don't want to."

Did she? She wasn't sure. She stabbed a piece of lettuce, swirled it around in the Italian dressing. In the far recesses of her mind, the dying cries for help stirred to life. A shiver of dread threaded down her spine.

Nic remained silent but she felt his gaze on her, steady, patient and compassionate.

"I survived," she murmured, plain and simple, almost hard. "They didn't."

Nic carefully laid aside his fork. "You were with them then?"

"In the same building. They were on the bottom floor. I wasn't." The lasagna began to lose its flavor. She didn't know why she'd started talking about this. She pressed a hand to her stomach.

Chair legs scraped loudly against the tile as Nic moved his chair closer to hers. "Hey."

With a touch gentle enough for Alex, he smoothed a hand over her head, letting it rest on the ends of her hair. His empathy throbbed between them, both surprising and welcome.

"You were alone in a collapsed building? How long? What happened?"

Throat tight, she swallowed. "About two days. In the dark. Under bricks and rubble."

The implication pulsed in the room, broken only by the sound of Alex's movements.

Now that she'd begun, she needed Nic to know. Maybe then he'd understand her fear and leave her alone. Maybe she could scare him away.

More than that, she needed to talk about the unspeakable. No one, not one person had ever listened all the way through.

"I couldn't see or move," she said, in a voice that sounded oddly detached. "But I could hear things falling and shifting, and I could hear the cries and moans."

"Others in the building?"

She nodded. The light pressure of Nic's fingers against her hair encouraged her. He listened with such intensity, she could almost believe he cared.

"After a while, the sounds faded away." She'd known somehow in her ten-year-old mind that the people around her were dead. Terrified, she'd called for her parents. They never answered.

"You had to be scared." He stroked her hair again. "So scared."

"I was. The smoke was the worst. I could smell it growing thicker and thicker but I could never see any flames. I kept thinking I would be burned alive with no means of escape. Later I discovered the fires had been far away in another section of the city. Wind had carried the smell everywhere."

But the scent of smoke stayed with her, a haunting kind of torture made worse by the loss of her sister.

"How did you get out?"

"Rescue workers heard me crying. I was transported back to the States. My parents were found later, but Grandmother never shared the details." For years she'd harbored the fantasy that her parents had survived and would be coming for her.

"First your parents and now your sister," Nic murmured softly. "No wonder you're overprotective of Alex."

"Everyone I love dies, Nic." She turned her face, saw her pain reflected in Nic's dark eyes. "I don't understand why I'm still here and they're all gone."

She hadn't meant to say the words, but they were true. Why had God spared her but taken everyone else?

"Not everyone, Cass." Nic gestured toward Alex who had rolled onto his back and was happily exploring his upraised feet. "Maybe you're here to raise that little boy the way your parents and your sister would have wanted."

"That's the only thing I can think of. But his own parents would have done a better job than I'm doing."

"Don't sell yourself short." He leaned closer. Cassidy's pulse ratcheted up a notch. Nic had the softest eyes. She swallowed, suddenly nervous about the expression she saw in those espresso depths. Before she could think of a reason to move away, Nic reached out and brushed back a loose strand of her hair. His fingers grazed her cheek, a rough-gentle touch that raised goose bumps.

"I think," he said, "that you are one strong, amazing woman and Alex is a lucky little boy to have you in his corner."

At the gentle words, tears formed, threatening to spill over. She didn't need this. Couldn't bear to let go in front of Nic.

She used the mention of Alex as an excuse to escape the throbbing emotion.

"The baby," she said lamely.

Before Nic could assure her that Alex was fine, she pushed away from the table, breaking contact with Nic's eyes and fingertips. As she reached for her sister's baby, Cassidy suffered from an uncomfortable truth. Maintaining an emotional distance from her new neighbor might not be as easy as she'd hoped.

## Chapter Eight

Study. He had to study.

Nic kicked back in the brown leather recliner commandeered from his brother Adam's overcrowded apartment and propped an enormous medical tome on his chest. A double jolt of java waited at his elbow for those times when he went cross-eyed.

Moving out on his own was going well so far. The apartment looked pretty good with its hodgepodge of furnishings donated by family and friends, all of whom dropped by on a regular basis. Too regular for a guy who wanted to secretly cram for his medical school entrance exam.

Today, everyone assumed he was out of town. He hadn't exactly lied to anyone, but he'd hinted at a rock-climbing expedition with a couple of his firefighter buddies. Anything to get some peace and quiet so he could study. Grateful, he bowed his head to the book.

He read two pages about synapses and ganglions before his mind wandered to Cassidy. She occupied his thoughts way too much lately.

She'd gotten to him the other night when she'd told him

about her parents. He had thought his heart would rip right through his T-shirt when she'd talked about being buried alive. As a firefighter, one of the worst fears and the most planned for scenarios was the danger of collapsing buildings. But he'd never lived through it. She had. Worse yet, she'd been a child, alone and scared and trapped.

He hadn't been blowing smoke when he'd told her she was amazing. Her faith amazed him, too. He'd heard people with far less heartache rage against God for their troubles. Cassidy had never done that. She'd questioned, but she'd stood strong.

Watching Cassidy over the past few weeks had got him to thinking about his own relationship with God. It wasn't that he didn't believe. He did. But his brothers claimed he was riding on his parents' prayers instead of his own. He didn't know about all that but it was food for thought.

He sighed and dragged a hand down his face.

How was he supposed to study when the orange blossom smell of Cassidy's hair, the silky texture of it beneath his fingers, kept intruding?

The woman didn't even like him.

He'd wanted to comfort her, had been sorely tempted to kiss her, but she'd bolted like a startled deer.

After all she'd told him, one thing stuck in his peanut brain like a thorn, and he'd turned it over and over inside his head. While she was trapped, she'd smelled smoke and feared burning alive. Then a house fire had taken her sister. He'd also noticed a smoke detector in every room in her apartment.

Could Cassidy be fire-phobic? Was this why she jumped every time he got close?

Nah. The notion didn't make sense. He didn't cause fires. He prevented them, put them out. She should feel safe with him, not threatened.

Firefighters were the good guys. That's why he loved his job.

The medical book grew heavy in his hands. He stared down at it. Yeah, well, he loved being a firefighter, but he'd love being a doctor, too. Time to get serious.

He started reading again, revisiting scientific principles, absorbing as fast and as much as he could. When brain overload threatened, he paused to ponder all he'd studied and to sip the cold, stout coffee.

Contrary to popular belief, his IQ was greater than his shoe size. Some folks would be shocked to know that.

He chuckled and rotated his neck left and right, listening to the crackles. Without giving it much thought he cataloged the anatomy of a neck ache. The upper portion of the trapezius as well as the levator scapula had stiffened to create tension, thereby contracting against cervical vertebra one through four.

Movement past his front window caught his attention. He turned his head, grimacing at the stiffness, and then sat up straight. The recliner emitted a metallic pop. His feet hit the wood floor with a thud.

Was that Cassidy?

He jogged to the door and yanked it open. Sure enough, his gorgeous neighbor was journeying down the sidewalk pushing a familiar navy-blue stroller complete with an alert, bright-eyed baby. Nic's mood elevated and he hadn't even looked at the white mood bowl.

"Hey, lady."

She turned toward him, the movement catching the light in her sun-drenched hair. She was dressed in running clothes, complete with classy sunglasses and a bright-blue headband.

He didn't know a single woman who compared with her. Or at least with the way he felt around her. The rest were friends, contrary to another popular myth. Friends with Cassidy was a start, but there was something else going on there, too.

Nic got a funny feeling beneath his rib cage. He must have fried his brain on the books.

Cassidy pushed the shades up on top of her head, a classy, movie-star action. "Nic, I thought you were gone for the weekend."

She was paying better attention than he'd suspected. Nice.

He struck a casual pose, leaning on the edge of his open front door. "Changed my mind. I had some study—" Nic caught himself in time. "—stuff to do."

He wasn't ready to admit his med-school failings to a woman he wanted to impress.

The thought startled him, but once it had taken form he realized it was true. Weird. He'd have to figure that one out later.

"Oh," she said. "You're busy. I guess I shouldn't keep you then."

Was that disappointment lurking behind that beautiful smile?

He pushed off the door and sauntered outside. The bright May morning drew him almost as much as the woman and child. "Where are you headed?"

"For a run. This stroller has worked out great." She patted the shiny metal handle. "Did I say thank you for thinking of this?"

The jogging stroller had been a brilliant idea, even if he *had* thought of it himself. His sister-in-law owned one and he'd known it was the answer for Cassidy's need to run and still be with Alex. He'd given the gift the other night when she'd told him about her parents, a stroke of genius that had broken the bizarre tension between them.

"About a dozen times, but guys like gratitude. Go ahead and thank me again."

She bent to adjust the awning over Alex's face, but not before Nic saw the gleam of humor. He crouched next to the baby to say hello. Alex flopped both arms and grinned.

"Things must be going better with Alex," he said.

He wanted to ask about the other night, to make certain he hadn't crossed some invisible line, but he didn't. Not yet. Sooner or later, he'd bring up the topic again. If she'd developed a phobia of fire, he wanted to know.

"We're getting there. Slowly." She grimaced but there was humor behind it. "Very slowly."

He squinted up at her. "The fact that you have enough energy to run again must mean something."

"True. Your mom reminded me that exercise energizes. And that I have to take care of myself in order to take care of Alex." When he frowned, confused by her mention of his mother, Cassidy went on. "Didn't she tell you I've called her a few times?"

"No." And he felt a tad annoyed that she hadn't. But then, he hadn't been hanging around the home place as often lately, either.

"Your mother has truly been an answer to my prayers. I've never met anyone quite like her. She even prayed with me on the phone one day when I was in a panic over a rash on Alex's bottom." She bit her bottom lip and looked away. "You're blessed to have a mother like her."

Nic thought of the times around the kitchen table when both his parents had counseled and prayed with him about some problem or another. Now he understood how fortunate he'd been. Cassidy hadn't had that.

"Family can be a pain, but yeah, they're a blessing, too."

"She invited me to have dinner with your family tomorrow after church."

Nic perked up. Sunday dinner with the fam was sounding good. "Are you coming?"

Her mouth tilted at the corners. "I said yes."

"I think I'm offended," he said lightly, though truth lurked behind the words. "You wouldn't go when *I* invited you."

"Your mother has helped me a lot. She's a wise woman."

He turned both index fingers to point at himself. "And I, her son, am a wise guy."

As he'd intended, Cassidy laughed. She bumped his foot with the toe of her shoe. "Are you ever serious?"

He thought of the MCAT book waiting inside.

"You would be surprised." He chucked Alex under the chin and rose to a stand. "Mind having some company on your jog?"

"I thought you had stuff to do."

"Stuff that can wait." He'd been up until two that morning cramming. A break was overdue. "We don't get many perfect days like this."

She glanced out at the street where cars sailed by, their metallic paint reflecting the bright sun. "Well…"

There she went again, throwing up barriers.

"Never mind. I don't want to intrude." He backed off and turned away, disappointed but annoyed, too. If she didn't want him around, fine. He wasn't exactly lonely.

"Nic." Her voice hesitated, uncertain.

He glanced over one shoulder, head tilted in question. It was her call.

She blinked twice and then smiled. "Got any running shoes?"

A grin started down in his belly, rose in his chest and landed on his face. He held up two fingers. "Two minutes."

Without analyzing the pure rush of pleasure, Nic hurried inside, donned running shoes and a Yankees cap and was back on the sidewalk in less than the allotted pair of minutes.

"Let's roll," he said and then laughed, looking at the stroller. Cassidy laughed, too. "No pun intended. Are we headed to Pride Park?"

"Yes." A block from the apartment was a park with a circular running track around the play area. They started in that direction. He crowded her out of the way and took over the stroller. The wheels clattered against the concrete walk. The baby's head bobbed and jostled, his eyes drooping with the rhythm.

"How are things at work? Catching up yet?"

"I wish." She didn't elaborate, a bad sign, he figured. Instead, she asked, "Why aren't you out with your friends this weekend?"

He looked at Alex and then at her, the grin in his belly still in full bloom. "I am."

Weird, but true. He was right where he wanted to be.

Cassidy got butterflies in her stomach when Nic said things like that. She knew he was teasing. He was always teasing. Notorious Nic's idea of fun could not be a stressed-out neighbor and her sometimes cranky nephew. From the gaggle of girls, and if she was fair, an equal group of guys, who had roamed in and out of Nic's apartment since he'd moved in, Cassidy was certain he could find better entertainment.

"My grandmother called again this morning," she said as they waited at the corner for the light to change.

"Sorry to hear that." A red sports car roared past, going far too fast. Nic braced an arm in front of her and scowled at the disappearing Camaro. "Dude. Slow down." To her he said, "Grandma still pressuring you?"

Cassidy wrinkled her nose at him. "Sometimes I wonder if she's right, if I'm cheating Alex out of a real family."

Easily pushing Alex's stroller with one hand, Nic took her elbow in the other and guided them across the busy street. "Don't do that. Don't sell yourself short."

"I want what's best for him."

"That would be you. *You* are a real family. Small but mighty." She was starting to believe him.

After they stepped up on the curb, Nic dropped his hold.

She realized then how protected and safe she'd felt for those few seconds. Notorious Nic was working his amazing charm on her and she couldn't seem to stop reacting to him.

She didn't understand the reaction, either. She had friends and a busy life. She didn't need Nic's attention.

After the other night when she'd told him things she'd never told anyone, he had been in her thoughts constantly. On the days he didn't bounce up to her apartment with some silly quip or tale of wild adventure or jokingly asking to borrow a cup of sugar, she missed him.

Dumb. Real dumb.

At times like this, she could forget he was a firefighter. Almost.

An hour later they returned to the apartment complex, drenched in sweat and laughing. Cassidy had never enjoyed a run in quite this manner. She'd raced Nic, beating him in a short sprint, though he'd cried foul, claiming the wheels on Alex's stroller gave her an unfair advantage. She'd laughed so hard, she'd had to sit down on the track, arms over upraised knees to get her breath. No doubt, he could have smoked her if he'd wanted to. The man was in amazing physical condition.

Nic had jogged forward, backward, sideways and around her in ever narrowing circles until he'd collapsed on the blacktop surface next to her, panting, the grin on his handsome face causing her exercise-pumped pulse to skitter. No wonder he could have any girl he wanted. Besides being darkly handsome, Nic was a ton of fun. She was working harder than ever to also remember that he had about as much substance as a dandelion puff. Somewhere along the line he'd put a dent in that strongly held opinion.

Dangerous. Very dangerous to be thinking of Nic as a solid

man with deep feelings and beliefs. He was a Christian. She'd gotten that much out of him during one of their late-night talks when Alex wouldn't sleep, she couldn't and Nic had chosen not to. Like most things, though, he didn't take his faith as seriously as she did.

"Come on in," he said when they reached his apartment door. "I have bottled water in the fridge."

"My kingdom for your water," she joked.

Nic lifted the stroller over the threshold and led the way. Once inside, he extracted Alex and sat him on the floor. "Is he okay here?"

Cassidy reached inside a pouch on the back of the stroller, took out several toys and placed them in front of the baby. "He is now."

"Make yourself comfortable. I'll grab that water."

She moved around the room, taking in the changes, hearing the suction of the refrigerator door and the clatter as Nic moved around.

"Everything looks different. I'm impressed."

A beige couch, a deep-maroon leather chair and a couple of occasional tables were set up around an interesting area rug in shades of beige, maroon and navy. All the boxes and stacks of household goods and clothes were gone.

"Did your girlfriends put everything away?"

"Friends who are girls. Let's get that part cleared up." He came around the recliner to hand her a bottle of cold water. "But no. I did everything myself."

"Even the wall hangings?" A clever assortment of photographs from Nic's various adventures had been grouped along one wall. The opposite wall held some sort of graphic design in colors that blended with the hodgepodge of furnishings. Her artistic eye found the choices intriguing.

She uncapped the bottle and took a long drink, letting the

cold chill the back of her throat. Condensation frosted the plastic and dampened her hand.

Taking his own bottle of water, Nic dropped onto the sofa. "Painted the design, too. Saw it on HGTV, but don't tell anyone." He patted the couch. "Sit. Cool down."

"What's the deal? Real men don't watch design shows."

"Right."

Amused, Cassidy sat, curling one foot beneath her. "Your secret is safe with me."

As she leaned her head back against the microfiber sofa and relaxed, a large, thick book that looked for all the world like serious study caught her attention. Curious, she leaned to pick up the text. It weighed a ton.

She read the title. "MCAT? Nic, what is this?"

Nic gulped half his bottle of water and then dragged the back of his hand across his mouth. His fingers froze in place as he realized what she was looking at.

"Pay no attention to that man behind the curtain," he said in a silly Oz-like voice.

"Nic, be serious." She hoisted the heavy textbook. "Is this yours?"

With a shrug, he tried to laugh it off. "Found it laying around. Thought I'd see if I could learn some big words to impress the girls."

"You're studying to take medical school entrance exams," she said in stunned wonder.

The completely incongruous concept ping-ponged around inside her head. Nic Carano studying to be a doctor? Notorious Nic? This was crazy.

"Nic? You are, aren't you?"

Nic responded by rubbing his temples and then dragging both hands over his face, which was now somber. "Promise me you'll keep this to yourself."

"Why? Nic, this is awesome, amazing."

"And surprising?"

"Well, yes, that, too. You don't exactly present yourself as the serious student type."

"Which is why I'd like to keep this between us, if you don't mind."

"No one else knows?"

He shook his head. "No one."

"Not even your family?" They were so close. Surely he'd told them.

"*Especially* my family."

She placed her half-empty bottle onto the coffee table and wiped a moist hand over her shorts. "I don't get it. Your family would be thrilled."

"That's the point. They'd be thrilled to know their baby boy, the son with mostly air in his head, was finally trying to make something of himself like the other kids have."

"Okaaay, forgive me, but I'm still not getting it." She leaned toward him. "Why wouldn't you want to share that with them?"

"I do. I want that more than I can tell you. When the time is right." He sucked in a lungful of air and blew it out slowly through pursed lips. "This won't be the first time I've taken the test." His eyebrows rose and fell in a wry facial shrug. "Or the second."

Understanding dawned. "Now I get it. You're afraid of failing again. Of letting them down."

"Bingo."

Nic looked so shaken by his admission that Cassidy couldn't help herself. She scooted closer and placed a hand atop his.

"How close were you to passing?"

Nic gazed down at where their hands touched, turned his palm up and laced his fingers with hers. The motion felt right.

Now Cassidy was the shaken one.

"Real close. I'm taking an online review class this time, plus the book study. Unless I'm a complete idiot I should do okay. But I can't just pass. I need good scores to get into the state programs."

This was a new side of Nic. Anyway, it was a side of him she'd tried not to see before. Now she realized the serious Nic had been there all along. This was the man, after all, who'd pulled Alex from a burning building, the man who'd sat by a strange baby's bed until a relative had arrived. A man who'd cheerfully rounded up baby furniture and clothes for a complete stranger.

"Your T-shirt lies," she said gently, still stunned by the wrenching paradigm shift. Her carefully held opinions of Notorious Nic, fueled by his self-deprecations were tumbling like stacked dominoes.

Puzzled, Nic's eyebrows came together before he dipped his chin and read the slogan on his shirt. "I took an IQ test. The results were negative."

With his usual humor, his lips twitched. "That remains to be seen."

Cassidy squeezed his fingers, felt him squeeze back. Funny how something as simple as holding hands could suddenly take on new meaning. She'd taken his hand to comfort him, as he'd comforted her that awful morning at the hospital and again the other night. Now that he'd let her past his facade of fun and games for a look into the complete Nic Carano, Cassidy had to face an unwanted truth.

She swallowed hard, her heart thudding in her throat at the stunning revelations going on inside her. Nic Carano was not only a lot of fun to be with, he was a much deeper guy than anyone suspected.

Trouble was, she didn't want him to be deep and complex.

Even though he might aspire to medical school, there was no guarantee he would make it. No guarantee he would trade a life-threatening job for a life-saving one. Worse yet, his entourage of girls called or texted him constantly.

She didn't need any of this in her already tumultuous life.

He squeezed her fingers again and smiled. Cassidy suffered a sinking sensation strong enough to leave a hole the size of the Grand Canyon.

She liked Nic Carano...far more than was prudent.

## Chapter Nine

The man was full of surprises.

On Sunday morning when Nic had shown up at her door dressed in a pale-yellow shirt and crisp navy slacks offering to drive her to church, Cassidy had nearly choked on her breakfast bar. All through the service, she was aware of him sitting too close, aware of the fresh scent of shower, shampoo and masculine warmth, aware of the timbre of his voice lifted in song.

Lord, forgive her. As hard as she fought it, he was definitely a distraction.

Now, here they were in the ample backyard of his family's home where she had received the most shocking surprise yet.

On arrival, Nic had introduced her to his family, some of whom she'd met. Altogether Nic had two sisters, Anna Marie and Mia, plus two brothers, Gabe and Adam. All except Adam were married with families, so an abundance of children ran around the backyard. She hadn't yet matched the children with their parents because every adult seemed equally interested in every child. A toddler boy with curly dark hair clung to Nic's leg. A little girl with the face of an angel sat atop Adam's broad shoulders, thrashing his back with a long weed and yelling, "Giddyap, horsie."

Several small ones ran in, out and between lawn chairs in a squealing game of freeze tag, while a couple of teenagers worked on a dilapidated go-cart turned upside down in the far corner of the yard. Occasionally, one of them called for help and one of the brothers or their father, Leo, jogged over for consultation.

Mia's husband, Collin, along with Leo and a slim young man named Mitch, manned the grill where the scent of hamburgers sizzled in the air. The Carano brothers drifted past a few times to add friendly advice and insults before drifting off to other pursuits.

The ease with which Rosalie and Leo related to their children and grandchildren fascinated Cassidy. She'd never been this easy with her grandmother. No one seemed overly concerned about soiled clothes or too much noise. In fact, noise seemed to be the common denominator among the Caranos. Everyone talked at once, gesturing with expressive hands. Laughter punctuated the conversations like exclamation points. Somewhere a radio belted out contemporary music.

Nic played yard darts with a half dozen other people but occasionally wandered over to where Cassidy stood talking with Rosalie and Mia as they prepared a table full of food "for the masses," as Rosalie put it.

Once, Nic draped an arm over his mother's shoulder and kissed her cheek. In return, she patted his, the mother–son love a visible, lovely thing. Emotion surged inside Cassidy. Though she'd been young when her mother died, at times like these Cassidy remembered the feeling of being loved unconditionally. The longing for a warm, loving family of her own almost choked her.

"You taking good care of my neighbor?" Nic asked, eyeing both his mom and sister. This afternoon his bright red T-shirt proclaimed, "I'd give my right arm to be ambidextrous."

Mia, whose full, wide mouth seemed to either be smiling

or talking all the time, said, "We're telling her about your naughty childhood."

Nic drew back in pretend horror. "She'll have me evicted."

The full mouth laughed. "Remember what the Bible says. 'Be sure your sins will find you out.'"

"I," he declared dramatically, slapping one hand against his chest "am a dead man."

With a teasing wink at Cassidy, he snitched a strawberry from the fruit plate Mia was arranging. She slapped his fingers. He drew back with a laugh. "Mom, Mia hit me."

Rosalie handed him another strawberry and shooed him back to his game.

"See what I have to put up with," she said, fondly gazing after her baby boy. "He likes you a lot, I'm thinking, Cassidy."

Her stomach dipped. "Nic likes all the girls."

"Mmm. Or maybe *they* like *him*. You may be surprised to know he's never been serious with anyone."

Actually, she was surprised, but she said, "Nic is rarely serious."

As soon as she said the words, she realized they were neither fair nor entirely true. They were the stereotypical Nic, not the real one. Sure, Nic knew how to have a good time and he could be wild and crazy, but she'd met the real man beneath the flash and dash.

The notion that Notorious Nic had never had a serious relationship was…interesting, to say the least.

"He went to church with you today," Mia said. "Do you know how long it's been since he's done that?"

Cassidy shook her head, remembering how distracted she'd been by the handsome man seated next to her. "He doesn't go with you?"

"Not in a while. He claims his job interferes, and I'm sure it does. But Nic has drifted." Rosalie's dark doe eyes saddened. "It breaks my heart to see one of my children ambivalent about the Lord."

It bothered Cassidy, too, but she got the idea Nic was searching to find his own way instead of leaning on his parents' faith. She couldn't fault him for that.

"Did you know," Rosalie went on, "that you are the first girl he's ever brought to a family gathering?"

Cassidy nearly dropped the tomato she was slicing. "You can't mean that."

"On my family's honor." Rosalie touched her heart.

Mia grinned at Cassidy. "The look on your face is priceless."

"I—" Cassidy blinked rapidly, trying to make some sense of the revelation. "I'm not sure what that means."

Rosalie patted her shoulder. "It means, dear child, that my wayward boy has feelings for you. I've been praying for a beautiful Christian woman to come along and give him a reason to settle down."

Cassidy managed a shaky laugh. Rosalie had no idea how impossible a relationship between her and Nic was. "Nic is attached to Alex. Not me."

Rosalie slid a spoon into a bowl of sliced melon, dark eyebrows drawing together in question. "You don't like my Nic?"

"Well, yes, of course I do. He's great." *He's funny and warm and generous. He's even changing diapers now.*

*Oh dear.*

The man in question jogged toward her. Cassidy's pulse danced a jitterbug, an effect she blamed on Rosalie's insinuations.

He reached out and snagged her hand. "Come on, Cass. I'm getting cremated in this game. I need a partner."

As his strong, firefighter's fingers wrapped around hers, the word *partner* took on an entirely new meaning.

\* \* \*

"What do you think of this one?"

A few days later, Cassidy still had Nic Carano on the brain, but tonight she was trying to concentrate on the teen group gathered at her place.

Cassidy spun sideways in her rolling desk chair to look at the freckled teenager. Angie leaned over the computer to peruse the design Cassidy had created for her MySpace page.

"I love it. You're good at this, Cassidy."

With a laugh Cassidy said, "Considering this is my bread and butter, I'd better be."

She didn't add the bitter truth that her career had taken a turn for the worse lately. No use worrying her Bible study girls. Regardless of her boss's expectations, Cassidy had come to the conclusion that she wanted a life outside her career. If that meant cutting back, she'd have to do it. Alex was her life now. Her career was not. Unfortunately, Shane Tomlinson was not at all happy to hear of her newfound dedication.

Angie, purple highlights in her hair shining under the light, twisted toward the six other girls lounging around the kitchen table. "Come look at the cool page Cassidy created for me."

Cassidy listened to the oohs and ahhs of the teens. Tonight was the first time in the more than a month since her sister's death that she'd resumed the weekly Bible study with the girls from her church. In truth, the meeting was more of a Christian mentoring group than anything, though she always presented a short, relevant lesson from scripture. By spending quality time listening to the girls, she'd been delighted to watch them grow as Christians.

In the process, she'd grown herself. Though she still questioned the losses, she'd felt the love and compassion and peace of God surrounding her with such sweetness. And He'd sent people into her life—people like the Caranos—when she'd needed them the most.

The Caranos. Once more, her mind drifted to last Sunday and the pleasant afternoon she'd spent with Nic and his big Italian-American family. They were the kind of family she and Janna had longed for all their lives. The kind of family she wanted to give to Alex but couldn't.

Her gaze went to the baby happily being passed from one girl to the next. Alex babbled something in her direction. Love bubbled up inside Cassidy. She'd been busy and active before he came along, but Alex had added a new, unexpected element of joy. As difficult as the adjustment was, she couldn't imagine her life without him now.

"It's so cool of you to do this for us," one of the other girls said, breaking her train of thought. "Will you change mine next week?"

"Sure, if we have time."

Cassidy had never told them, but she designed their online pages not only for their enjoyment, but as a means to monitor what was going on in their lives. Over the past year, she'd been able to head off some trouble areas for a couple of the girls and to talk to them about inappropriate visitors to their pages.

"Someone's coming up the stairs." Angie started toward the door. "Maybe it's Melissa."

Cassidy, too, was concerned about the absent Melissa. According to evidence on her MySpace page, Melissa was hanging around with a questionable crowd.

"How can you hear footsteps with all this chatter going on?" she asked.

Almost before Cassidy finished the question, Angie opened the door and Nic breezed inside.

"Whoa," he said, skidding to a stop. "Is this a party?" He

smiled, accenting the dimple in his chin. "And why wasn't I invited?"

Seven teenagers giggled, turning wide-eyed, speculative gazes on Cassidy. The heat of a blush climbed up the back of her neck.

That day at the cookout, Rosalie and Mia had put the craziest thoughts in her head. Thoughts that hammered away at her, threatening to undermine her resolve to remain emotionally distant from a guy with two strikes against him.

Nic didn't help matters in the least. The fact that he was a firefighter was offset by his application to med school. If he got accepted, he would no longer be a fireman and, therefore, no longer be in imminent danger. She could actually date him without fear.

As soon as the thought arrived, she cast it down, aghast. Fireman or not, he would still be Notorious Nic.

Or would he?

To make matters more unsettling, their relationship had changed dramatically since she'd discovered his fear of failure and the secret longing to please his family. Who would have thought Nic Carano, the man who faced raging fires, ziplined in Mexico and had once ridden a Brahma bull, would be afraid of anything? The notion tugged at her heart.

So much so that she'd even spent several hours this week sitting at his kitchen table, drilling him on terms she could barely pronounce. Behind the smoke and mirrors, Nic was a very bright man.

Add to that the innuendos from his family and Cassidy was one confused *chica.*

"Nic," she said, a little too breathlessly, a little too happy to see him considering they'd jogged together yesterday. "I thought you were on duty tonight."

"Excuses, excuses. I traded shifts with a buddy who needs

off tomorrow. His wife is scheduled to have a baby." Without missing a beat, he dazzled the girls with a wink and another smile as he whisked Alex into his arms. Holding the baby at arm's length, he wiggled the chubby body back and forth saying, "Hey partner, what's shakin'?"

Mouth wide with pleasure, Alex drooled. Cassidy rose, grabbed a tissue and swiped.

"You're getting good at this." Nic beamed at her.

Foolishly, she beamed back. "You know what they say about practice."

"Too late. You were already perfect."

The hum of speculation around them grew louder.

In self-defense, Cassidy introduced Nic to each of the girls. They simpered and cast sideways glances at each other.

Fighting not to roll her eyes, Cassidy said to her neighborly intruder, "Did you need something, Nic? Or are you only passing by?"

They both laughed at the inside joke. Nic had started it when he wanted an excuse to come up for a visit, though the only reason to climb those particular stairs was to arrive at her apartment.

"Passing by, hoping to take you and Alex out for ice cream." Alex grabbed hold of his ear. Nic paid him no mind. "I need to talk to you about something."

Cassidy studied Nic's face, trying to gauge what he was not saying. This was his serious side. She was beginning to recognize the difference. "Can I take a rain check on the ice cream and come down later to talk?"

"Works for me. I'm not going anywhere."

"No company?"

He grinned. "Only you."

A skitter of awareness danced through her, both happy and anxious. She grinned back, glad that Rachel and Mandy and

Nic's usual gaggle of female company had been nowhere around for the last week.

She cocked a hip. "Got popcorn?"

"Theater butter, guaranteed to clog your arteries."

"EMT to the rescue?" What in the world was she doing? Flirting?

"CPR could be called for at any time." He pumped his eyebrows. His gaze dropped to her mouth. "I'm good with that."

She imagined he was. The thought of kissing Nic tingled every nerve ending in her body.

The ripple of giggles from the teenagers brought Cassidy back to reality. Goodness. Nic was causing her to lose her sense of decorum.

"Go away, Nic."

He chuckled knowingly, but handed Alex to the nearest teenager and backed toward the door. "See ya."

After the door closed behind him, Cassidy almost wilted into the carpet.

The teens attacked like a friendly school of sharks. A volley of mingled comments shot at her.

"Are you dating him? He's a hottie. Like a movie star or something. That dimple in his chin made my knees weak. Why didn't you tell us about him? Are you in love?"

"Girls, stop!" She held her hands against her hot cheeks, laughing but embarrassed, too. "Nic is my neighbor. My friend."

"Oh, right. That's why you went all dreamy-eyed when he walked in."

"Yeah, and did you see the way he looked at her?" Angie wiggled her fingers as though she'd touched something hot. "Ooh-la-la!"

"We know flirting when we see it."

Cassidy gave up and let them speculate.

How could she be expected to explain her feelings for Nic when she didn't understand them herself?

When the last of the teenagers left, Cassidy glanced at the sunburst clock above the couch. The hour was later than she'd expected and it was almost time to put Alex down for the night. A consistent routine, she'd discovered, made a world of difference. But she'd promised Nic.

"Want to go see Notorious Nic?" she said to Alex. The little dude, as Nic called him, bicycled his arms and legs with enthusiasm as if he understood.

With Alex against her shoulder she trotted down the steps to apartment seventeen. The door opened before she knocked.

"I saw the girls leave," he said by way of explanation.

"Thank goodness," she joked. "I was starting to think you could see through walls."

"Does this mean I've reached superhero status?" He leaned forward to nuzzle Alex under the chin. Having Nic this close brought back her wayward thoughts.

She ignored his question as a buzz of energy danced between them. Nic must have noticed, too. He lifted his face from Alex but didn't move away. Dark, dark eyes studied her. Serious eyes.

The jitters in her belly got worse.

"Where's my popcorn?" she managed, dismayed by the breathless sound of her voice.

Nic backed off, a funny quirk to his lips. "Coming right up. Grab a seat while I stick the bag in the nuker. You want a Coke?"

Cassidy kissed Alex on the forehead, laid him on the play mat that had recently appeared in Nic's apartment without explanation and followed Nic into the kitchen area. "Too late for caffeine. How about water?"

"Works for me, too." He motioned toward the fridge. "I'm on shift tomorrow. Gotta get up early."

"Tap water is fine. We'll save the bottles for running."

"We. I like the sound of that."

"Don't get cocky. I only let you come along to entertain Alex." She cast a quick glance at the baby. He was doing mini-push-ups and drooling on a terry-cloth fire truck.

The popcorn began to pop, the scent filling up the apartment. Nic sniffed the air. "Man, I love that smell." When the microwave *pinged,* he removed the bag, holding it by the top with the tips of his fingers. "Hot, hot. Good thing there's a firefighter on the premises."

The comment cooled Cassidy's enthusiasm. She wished he wouldn't remind her of the primary reason why she shouldn't be here. He was on duty tomorrow. Anything could happen.

She found a glass bowl in the upper cabinet and held it out while he dumped the popcorn. "What did you need to talk to me about?"

Nic's hands paused on the now empty bag. "In a minute. Wait until we sit down."

A worse feeling crept over Cassidy.

Nic blew into the popcorn bag, twisted the top and slammed his hand against the bottom. *Pop!* Even though she'd seen it coming, Cassidy jumped.

She jabbed an index finger toward him. "If Alex starts crying, you've lost your superhero status."

Nic peered over at the child who seemed unfazed by the unexpected noise. "Superhero status, huh? So now you admit it."

"I admit nothing." Pretending haughtiness, she pitched a piece of popcorn into her mouth before going to the couch.

Nic settled close. Real close. Cassidy knew she should probably scoot away but she didn't want to. Not yet anyway.

"Alex is trying to sit up alone now," she said, more for

something to fill the silence than to start a conversation about baby development.

"I noticed. It's kind of cute when he topples over."

She chuckled. "I know. It's like watching slow motion. One minute he's up, and then slowly, slowly he leans sideways."

"The leaning tower of Alex." Nic tossed a piece of popcorn into the air and caught it in his mouth.

Cassidy applauded, making fun. "A man of many talents."

He aimed at her. When she didn't open her mouth, he tossed anyway. The popcorn bounced off her chin.

They both laughed.

"Nic, this is fun, but I can't stay long. I need to get up early in the morning and try to get some work finished before I go to the office."

"Still behind?"

"Yes. And my boss is not a happy camper. He says I'm ruining my career."

"Are you?"

"I don't know. I love my work but it doesn't consume me like before. My mind is in a dozen places instead of totally focused on the job."

"Life isn't all about work."

The comment was something she would have expected from Nic before, but now she knew his goal and the efforts he'd taken to reach it. "Let's don't talk about this. Tell me why you wanted me to come down."

"All right." He pressed both palms against his thighs, shoulders arching before reaching for a piece of paper on the end table next to his medical guide. "Got this today."

"What is it?" She leaned forward and saw the words *fire marshal* across the top. Dread pulled at her insides. She must have gasped because Nic snagged her gaze with his.

"You asked to see the report when it came in."

She nodded, unable to speak just yet. With each passing day the grief had settled more and more into a deep, abiding ache instead of screaming agony. Yet, not a day went by that she didn't remember the fire that had stolen her sister and Alex's parents.

"Are you okay?" Nic touched her cheek, brought her gaze back to his. "Can you handle this?"

She nodded again, not sure at all.

"Cass," he said softly, studying her face. "Is it the memory of your sister or the idea of fire in general that upsets you most?"

Her lips went dry. "Both."

"Talking about fire scares you, doesn't it?"

She shuddered, suddenly cold though the room temperature was pleasant. "Terrifies me."

Nic's fingers trailed down her arm to grasp her hand. "For a while I thought it was me, but now everything makes sense. The smoke alarms in every room of your apartment, even the way you've tried to push me away."

"I didn't try—" But she couldn't lie. Nic was an intelligent man. He'd known she wanted to avoid him. "The problem isn't you."

"It's my job, isn't it?" Nic loosened his grip on her hand and leaned forward, elbows on his thighs, to stare at Alex. A subtle shift in mood had occurred that Cassidy didn't understand.

"Firefighting is dangerous, Nic. I'm glad you'd rather be a doctor."

Normally any hint that she might be concerned about him would instigate a wisecrack about his ego or some other sassy Nic remark. This time he let the opportunity slide and instead made a funny little huffing sound.

In a distant voice, he said, "Yeah. Good thing."

Several seconds ticked past while Cassidy contemplated

Nic's odd behavior. Alex flopped over on his back and gurgled, a reminder of the time. The baby needed to be in bed. So did she.

Though she had no great desire to hear the ugly details of her sister's death, she might as well get it over with. "Will you tell me about the report now?"

Nic's gaze flicked to her and then to the page in his hand. After a couple more seconds, he shook off the strange mood.

"The cause of the fire was pretty much what we thought. No arson or foul play. An electrical short. It started in the downstairs front bedroom."

Pain pierced Cassidy's heart. "Where Janna and Brad slept."

"Yes."

Cassidy closed her eyes, imagining the menacing flames that sucked the life from her only sibling. Her throat threatened to close. "No wonder they didn't have a chance."

"They didn't. That part's a mercy, Cassidy. As hard as it is to believe there could be good in this, that part is good. Toxic gas took them quickly."

The horror of such an insidious killer made her nauseous. Deadly fumes that sneaked up on her beautiful sister while she slept, dreaming happy dreams of her home and husband and baby.

"But why didn't the smoke detectors work?" she asked, tormented by that one thought. "I bought them myself. I helped Brad install them the day they moved in."

She'd tried so hard to keep her tiny family safe. Dear, accommodating Brad had thought she was overcautious and paranoid on the subject of fire, but he'd done the work on the spot to appease her.

"The one in Alex's room worked properly," Nic said. "I heard it myself. Someone had removed the battery from the one downstairs."

With a groan, Cassidy pressed a palm against her forehead. "Dear Lord, why? Why?"

But she knew why. Janna complained about the instrument's sensitivity. When she cooked certain foods, the alarm reacted.

"We'll never know for sure who disengaged the battery. Unfortunately, it's a common occurrence. We see it all the time. Let me tell you, finding a nonfunctioning smoke alarm makes a firefighter crazy."

"Me, too." That's why she had one in every room of her apartment and hanging over her desk at work. Brad and Janna had refused to be that "paranoid," they'd called it.

"Janna loved scented candles," she said, trying to piece together the truth that killed her sister. She shuddered. "I hate them. I begged her not to buy any at all, but she thought they were perfectly safe. She wouldn't burn one while I was there because she knew they upset me, but I know she used them. Vanilla," she said sadly. "The house always smelled of vanilla. Maybe one of them caused the alarm to sound so she took the battery out and forgot about it."

"Yeah, it's possible." Absently, Nic popped a knuckle. The sound was loud in the quiet room. "Whatever the reason, I'm sorry, Cass. For you, for Alex, for her. She was beautiful. Like you."

The sadness in Nic's remark shook her. She'd never considered that a tragic scene would also have affected him. She'd only considered how he reminded her of her sister's death. Not of how much he'd done, and how he'd tried to save her family.

"You carried her out," she murmured. "Oh, Nic. How awful for you."

His jaw tightened. He swallowed.

With mingled sorrow and gratitude, she touched his cheek. Their gazes collided.

"Hey," he said softly. "You're crying."

Cassidy hadn't realized she was, but now she felt the wetness rolling down her face. Unable to speak, she shook her head and tried to turn away. Nic would have none of it. He pulled her to him, pressed her cheek against the soft cotton of his silly T-shirt. His hand stroked the back of her hair, comforting.

"Cry if you need to, baby. You don't always have to be strong."

As if she'd needed permission, Cassidy let the tears come. Part of her wanted to feel foolish for the long overdue reaction to her sister's untimely death. Another part of her knew she needed this cleansing.

While Nic stroked her back and hair and murmured reassurances, she cried for her sister and Brad, for baby Alex's loss of his parents, for her own parents long dead.

When the siege ended, she remained in Nic's arms, reluctant to pull away. Funny how safe and comforted she felt in a fireman's strong, fit arms. No, not just any fireman's, but Nic's alone.

The thought was both scary and enticing.

Beneath her cheek, Nic's strong heart beat steady and sure. He smelled of cotton and popcorn and that special something that was Nic's alone. Something comforting and good.

"I'm okay now," she managed through a throat still clogged with emotion, the sound muffled against Nic's chest. She sniffed, a little embarrassed.

As she leaned back a tiny bit, Nic's hands slid around to cradle her face.

"Are you sure?" he asked, peering intently into her eyes.

She nodded shakily.

"Thank you," she whispered. "I needed that."

Nic's thumbs traced the tracks of her tears and stroked the corners of her mouth. Her lips tingled in response.

"You know what *I* need?" His voice was husky and warm.

Before she could venture a guess, he lowered his face, his breath a feather-touch against her lips. She knew in that instance he was going to kiss her.

Cassidy tried to think of all the reasons why he shouldn't. She tried...and failed.

## Chapter Ten

Fire Engine One swung around the tight corner on the return to the station. The inside reeked with the smell of burned rubber. The fire at the tire manufacturing company had taken hours to subdue, and even now one engine company remained on the scene to kill hot spots.

Nic glanced across the seat to his buddy, Sam Ridge. What he saw brought a laugh. "Man, you should see your face."

Black soot smeared his high cheekbones and rimmed his mouth and eyes.

Ridge's mouth twisted. "Can't be as bad as yours."

The captain, seated in the front, swiveled. "None of you boys are winning any beauty contests. Not even your women will recognize you."

His friend harrumphed but said nothing. Nic knew what the captain didn't. Ridge didn't have a woman, although plenty of ladies noticed his native good looks and long, athletic form. Nic knew his friend had reasons for steering clear of the female population. His wounds ran deep.

As for Nic, his thoughts immediately went to Cassidy. She'd freak out if she smelled this smoke and fire all over him.

He'd be sure to grab a shower and plenty of cologne before he jogged up the steps to bug her.

Cassidy. He smiled, aware that his teeth gleamed snow white against his sooty skin.

Last night, he'd kissed her. He'd thought of little else today to the point that his captain had commented on his quietness during the fire call. He, who usually jabbered and bounced around as hyper as a rat terrier, was struck dumb.

Nic wasn't sure what the big deal was. He'd kissed plenty of girls over the years, though if he admitted it, none in a while. Not since Cassidy and Alex began to occupy all his time as well as his thoughts. Kissing Cassidy was different, though. Not that he could put his finger on what that difference was.

Weird. He wasn't sure what was going on in his head or maybe in his heart, but one thing was for sure, he'd never felt this way about anyone else.

That fact made him a little nervous.

His cell phone ripped into his latest download, the creepy movie theme from *Jaws*. The sound always brought a smile to his lips and usually a shiver from the ladies. He kind of liked that.

Ridge shook his head and grinned before turning to look out the window.

Nic flipped open the instrument. "Party Central. Elvis speaking."

"Nic. Adam." His brother's tone was short and serious, not at all like Adam. Nic's radar went up.

"What's up, bro?"

"Got some bad news."

All the flippancy went out of Nic. He sat up straight, tensed by the sudden foreboding in the back of his mind. His brother wasn't one to exaggerate. "What's going on? Is everyone all right?"

By everyone, he meant family. Had there been an accident? One of the kids. Oh, please, God, not that.

"Mom's in the hospital."

"What?" His hands started to shake. "What happened? Did she have an accident?"

"Look, I'm sorry to tell you on the phone, but we're trying to get the word out. We need to start the prayer chain. Nonstop."

The words scared Nic even more. His throat tightened. Mom was the rock, the family hub, the one to whom everyone went with troubles. She couldn't get sick or hurt.

"Adam. Brother. What's the matter with our mama?"

A long pause pulsed through the phone. Nic was aware of passing cars, of people on the sidewalks, of Ridge and the captain staring at him, of the awful stench of burned rubber.

Finally Adam's strained voice said, "When your shift ends, come to the hospital. Nicky," he paused again and sucked in a quivering breath, "Mom's got cancer."

Cassidy carried an assortment of plastic shopping bags from the car to the apartment complex. Today was Saturday and she'd found great bargains in the baby section at Penny's. Alex was outgrowing clothes so fast she could barely keep up. Thanks to Mia and Anna Marie she had a few things but, in truth, she enjoyed shopping for Alex more than for herself.

"'Cause you're so cute," she said, kissing his chin. He responded by grabbing a hunk of her hair.

As she passed the walkway to Nic's apartment her attention was drawn to the dark window. He wasn't home. A frisson of disappointment shimmied through her. He'd been on duty last night. She'd expected him to sleep most of the day. Instead, he was gone. Probably out with friends.

The disappointment deepened, frustrating her. She hadn't seen Nic since he'd kissed her. She should have known their relationship was moving into the personal zone, but somehow she'd managed to ignore her feelings. She'd been bowled over by the avalanche of emotion one tender, achingly sweet kiss could generate.

She'd known from the beginning that a charmer like Nic had been her weakness in college. But she was sure she'd learned her lesson well. Now she worried about falling for another guy who could sweet-talk her into things she shouldn't do.

The idea frightened her. At the same time she wondered if she was being fair. He'd kissed her, not asked her to move in with him. Maybe she was overreacting.

But to Cassidy kissing was a big deal. As hard as it was to admit, she wouldn't mind kissing him again. And again.

At the top of the stairs she set her shopping bags on the landing to unlock the door and hoist Alex higher onto one hip. As she maneuvered the key into the lock with one hand, a car door slammed in the parking lot below. She glanced down to see Nic exit his truck. Her heart lurched.

Resolved not to behave like one of her Bible study teens, she pushed the door open and took Alex inside.

On the return trip for the bags her traitorous eyes searched for her neighbor, finding him. Something in the way he moved drew her attention. Plastic bags dangling from both arms, she leaned over the railing to observe.

Nic didn't walk with his usual jaunty step. He wasn't whistling or singing some silly song. Instead, he moved slowly as though his feet weighed a ton. He looked forlorn, depressed even.

The notion stunned her. Nic was a lot of things, but she'd never seen him depressed. Something was wrong.

All self-consciousness fled. She took the bags inside, changed Alex's diaper, washed his face and hands and then hurried downstairs.

Nic had been there for her, not once, but many times since the fire. If something was wrong, friendship demanded she return the favor.

The apartment was dark, but she knew he was in there. She banged on his door. "Nic. It's Cassidy."

A minute passed before he opened the door.

"You look awful," she blurted.

Some of his old humor gleamed for a few seconds. "Sweet talker."

She pushed past him, going into his living room where she turned to face him. His apartment smelled like reheated pizza.

"What's wrong? Can I help?"

Nic slowly closed the door, leaned there for a moment as if gathering strength before coming toward her. "Sit. I could use a friend right now."

Never taking her eyes off him, Cassidy lowered her body onto the couch. The firm cushion squeaked a tiny bit. She settled Alex onto her lap facing Nic, hoping the baby would cheer him.

As much as she hated knowing, she had to ask about his job. He had been on duty last night. Cassidy shuddered to think about it. "Did something happen at work? A bad fire?"

"No, no fire. It's my mom."

"Rosalie?" His answer shocked her. "Nic, what's wrong? Is she sick?"

"Yeah. Bad sick." He raked a hand down his face, rasping out a ragged breath. "Cass, she has breast cancer."

Blood drained out of Cassidy's head. She felt weak with the implications. Weak and frightened. What did one say in the face of such a terrifying diagnosis?

"Nic, I'm so sorry. What can I do? What do you need?" She grabbed one of his hands. "Anything. You name it."

His expression distraught, he shook his head. "I don't know. The family has a prayer chain."

"I'll pray. Every day, I promise. We will expect God to do something amazing. He will. I just know it." She knew prayer worked. It had sustained her more times than she could count, the most recent still ongoing. "Can we go see her?"

Absently, he jiggled Alex's outstretched hand, but Cassidy could see his mind was elsewhere.

"I just came from the hospital. The doctors came in and talked options. Scary stuff."

"How advanced is the cancer?"

"They're still testing to be sure, but the news is not good. Mom, I discovered, has known something was wrong for a while but didn't say anything to anyone but Dad. She's been to the doctor a lot this month." He stared down at his hands and then back up at her. "I didn't even know."

"She didn't want you to worry."

"But I should have noticed. I should have paid more attention. This is my mother!"

At the sharpness in Nic's tone, Alex started babbling like crazy and reached for him. This time Nic noticed. Almost desperately, Nic pulled the baby against his chest and clung to him in a way that pierced Cassidy's heart.

"I don't know what to do," he said to her over Alex's shoulder. "Mom's our anchor."

Hurting for him, Cassidy stroked his arm over and over again, trying to convey some sense of comfort. "Maybe it's your turn to be strong for her."

"Yeah. Yeah, I guess that's true." He rested his cheek against Alex's fuzzy blond head. "You know about being strong. You're a good example."

"Sometimes you don't have a choice."

"We always have a choice. You could have caved to the pressure from your grandmother."

"Yes, but look what I would have missed." She rubbed a

hand down Alex's back, the striped T-shirt rumpled beneath her fingers, the tiny jean shorts and soft denim shoes adorable. "The reward far outweighs the sacrifice."

"I'm afraid that won't be true this time." He moved the baby from his shoulder to his lap. Alex leaned forward to press his open mouth against Nic's knees, bobbing up and down. Nic's strong grasp held him safely even though the baby's bottom rose in the air. "I'm scared, Cass. What if she dies?"

"Medical science is doing amazing things today with breast cancer. I know several survivors." She took the straining baby from him and propped him between them on the couch. "And you know what else I know?"

He shook his head, looking at her through bloodshot eyes.

"I know a big, big God and so does your mother." She touched his cheek. "So do you, Nic. You should talk to Him about this."

"Yeah, I've been thinking about that, too."

"I can tell you from experience that He's there and He cares about your pain. For a while after the fire, I struggled to make sense of the senseless. I wondered why God had done such a thing, but finally my pastor helped me understand that God didn't kill my family. The Bible says Jesus came to give life, not to take it. He loves me. I'm His child. He wouldn't hurt me on purpose. Bad stuff just happens. There's no doubt about that, but Jesus is right here, longing to comfort and strengthen and carry you through this."

Nic bit his bottom lip and looked away, but not before she saw the yearning in his eyes.

She squeezed his hand, tears forming on her lids. "Will you let me pray with you?"

She'd prayed with her teen girls as a group but she'd never done this before. As self-conscious as she felt, Cassidy knew this was the right thing to do.

"It's been a while," he said softly. "Do you think He'll listen to a prodigal son?"

She laced her fingers with his. "I have no doubt at all."

Later that evening, Nic returned to the hospital. This time Cassidy went along. He was still scared out of his mind and disappointed that Cassidy's prayer hadn't automatically fixed the problem. But he'd watched Cassidy come from shattered despair to strong resolve and finally to peace. Tragic circumstances hadn't broken her. They had made her stronger.

God, she claimed, had been there for her in those awful hours when neither she nor Alex could sleep, when she feared that she didn't have the ability to mother a child, when the weight of dealing with funerals and autopsy reports and grief had threatened to drown her.

All his life, he'd been surrounded by believers and a Christian family with rock-solid faith, but Nic hadn't given God much thought in a long time. For as long as he could remember he'd been taught that God was the answer to every need. Somewhere along the line, he'd drifted away, too busy with enjoying life to think about God. It seemed like a sorry deal to run to Him now, asking for help and maybe even a miracle. Cassidy assured him the Lord didn't care about the circumstances. He simply wanted to help His children as a loving parent would.

And boy, did Nic need help now.

He pushed open the door to his mother's hospital room and waited until Cassidy, carrying Alex on her hip, passed through, her orange blossom scent tickling his nose. Much more pleasant than hospital smells.

The whole Carano gang was here again, jammed into the small space like Italian sausages.

Mama was propped up in a hospital bed, looking far too

healthy to be stuck between white sheets with an IV dripping into one arm. The sight knotted his gut. He wanted to throw up.

"Don't come in here with that long face, Nicholas Alexander," his mother said.

Cassidy shot him a funny look. He'd never told her his middle name was the same as Alex's first one.

"How ya doing, Mom?" he asked.

"Better than you. Come here." Rosalie raised her free arm.

Nic bent to receive her embrace, his heart hammering into his throat. He wrapped his arms around her shoulders and held her for several seconds, absorbing the moment, the fleshy softness and ever-present bakery smell of his mother. He thought of all the hugs he'd taken for granted over the years, forgotten even. Never again. Every moment with her was precious now that he had to face the fact that even she was not immortal.

"I love you, Mom," he whispered.

She patted his cheek. "I know you do. I love you, too. Have you had supper? You look tired. Dad brought sandwiches and pastry from the bakery."

Nic laughed. Leave it to his mother to make sure everyone was fed even from her hospital bed. "We'll eat later."

Rosalie motioned to Cassidy who hung back at the foot of the bed, a gentle smile curving her lips. If she felt out of place with his family, she didn't show it. And he'd never been so glad to have her company as he was tonight.

"Cassidy, make him eat. He's too thin." Mom shifted in the bed, her body whispering against the linens. "Mia, hand that platter around. Gabe, we need drinks."

"This isn't a picnic, Mom," Nic reminded her.

"Why not? We're all here. Food's here." She gestured around the room, a smile dancing in her dark eyes. "In Carano language that means, let's party."

He knew what she was doing and he loved her for the

effort. Mom never wanted anyone to worry about her. Family was her everything.

With a jolt, he realized he'd been trying to run away from the very thing that mattered most in life—his family's love and care and interest.

"She's right, gang." He clapped his hands once, rubbing them together for good measure. Though his heart wasn't in it, if Mama wanted a family party, he'd give her one. "Gabe, you buy the drinks."

"I figured as much," Gabe grumbled in jest. "I pay. You eat. Right?"

"That's the way the system works, bro," he said, determined to liven things up for his mother's sake. "Adam will go with you to the machines in case you run out of money."

Adam shot his father a grin. "Dad comes, too. He's the one with the fat wallet."

Leo, whose stricken expression had begun to abate with the banter between his boys, patted his back pocket. "I knew I should have left this at home. My sons become rich lawyers and they still pick my pockets."

Nic squelched a flare of envy. Dad never missed a chance to brag about his successful lawyer sons. Someday maybe he'd have reason to be proud of Nic, as well.

"Go, go, you silly men." Rosalie shooed them with both hands. "A person could starve to death while you argue."

The grim reminder of death, even in jest, dampened Nic's spirits. He forced a grin as his brothers and father disappeared into the hallway.

"Come on, ladies." He grabbed a wad of latex gloves from the box next to his mother's bed and handed one to Cassidy and his sisters. "Blow these up. We need balloons."

Rosalie wiggled her fingers toward the baby in Cassidy's arms. "Let me have that little one for a while."

Cassidy handed over the baby, who stared around in interest at the unfamiliar surroundings while Rosalie clucked and cooed at him.

Holding the floppy glove to her lips, Cassidy blew until the fingers filled and stuck straight up. All the while, her heart ached for Nic. Playing to the opinion that he was the clown, the never serious son, Nic broke into full party mode, joking, teasing, filling the room with an energy she knew he didn't feel.

She was the only one present that knew he was taking the MCAT again tomorrow morning, bright and early. He'd intended to study tonight. Now she wondered how he would concentrate on the exam when his mind and heart were here in this room with his mother.

"Woody Woodpecker." Nic grabbed her glove balloon and scrubbed a red marking pen over the protruding fingers. He added two huge eyes and a wide, smiling mouth. "See?"

His mother laughed and his sisters groaned.

He was shattered, devastated by his mother's illness, but if they wanted a party Notorious Nic came on the scene and gave them one.

The beauty of that kind of love made Cassidy want to cry.

It also made her feel something deep in her heart that she had never intended to feel. Something strong and sweet, lovely and fearsome.

And she had no idea what to do about it.

## *Chapter Eleven*

Rain pounded the window next to Cassidy's bed. Lightning flickered, followed by a rolling boom of thunder.

Over the baby monitor she heard Alex begin to cry. With a sigh, Cassidy rolled over for a look at her alarm clock. The number four glowed red. She groaned aloud. Alex had been doing much better, usually sleeping until six, but the storm must have wakened him.

The crying grew louder. She cocked her head to listen. Though he was probably hungry, this cry sounded different. He must be scared. Poor lamb.

Cassidy shoved back the sheet and padded through the dark apartment into the nursery. The angel night-light glowed, guiding her inside.

"Shh, darling boy, I'm here. Shh." She switched on the small, dim lamp next to the changing table, blinking for a few seconds. In the shadowy room, the baby-scented air hung cool and damp. Thunder rattled the windows. Lightning flickered like flames of fire across the floor.

Cassidy's nerves jittered. Nic was on duty tonight.

As she lifted the baby from the crib he quieted, but a new worry eclipsed all others.

"You're hot." She frowned and pressed a cool hand against his forehead. Too hot.

After carrying him to the changing table, Cassidy took his temperature and replaced his wet diaper. He fussed, whimpering, almost a moan. The sound frightened her.

Holding the thermometer toward the lamp, she squinted at the digital readout. "One hundred and one point four."

Her mind worked, trying to remember the books she'd read. Was that high for a baby? Was it in the danger zone? She knew normal but how high was high?

For a moment, she considered phoning Rosalie. Then, with a heavy heart, she remembered. Even she had come to count on the wisdom and strength of the Carano matriarch. Little wonder the hospitalization and diagnosis were so difficult for Nic and his siblings. She had to believe Rosalie with her valiant spirit and powerful faith would beat the disease.

Alex started to cry harder. Though he was hot, his skin prickled in the cool night air. Cassidy quickly slid his feet and arms into a pair of cotton pajamas and then hurried to the telephone. With the receiver in hand, she paused. Who could she call? It was far too late to contact anyone except Nic and he was on duty. Even if he knew what to do, he couldn't rush to her rescue this time.

Finally, she phoned the hospital emergency room and spoke to a nurse who advised her to give the baby some acetaminophen and take him into the pediatrician's office in the morning if he didn't improve. Not especially comforted, but somewhat relieved, Cassidy did as the woman suggested, fixed Alex a fresh bottle and sat down to rock him. At times like this, she realized why God intended for children to have two parents. Moral support took on an entirely new meaning at four o'clock in the morning.

The minutes crawled on while outside the storm raged. Thunder rumbled like a distant airplane. Lightning flickered through the blinds, illuminating the baby's fretful expression. Cassidy rocked and prayed. At seven, Alex's temperature had not improved but he'd fallen into a fitful slumber.

After placing him in the crib, she reached for the telephone once more, this time dialing her boss. He wasn't going to be happy but she had no choice.

"Shane, this is Cassidy Willis."

"Yes?" The art director's voice was cool.

"I won't be in to work this morning. Maybe not this afternoon, either. Alex is sick."

A long silence hummed through the receiver. Cassidy's fingers tightened. Her boss had been less than cordial of late. "Shane, are you still there?"

"I heard you, Cassidy." A loud sigh expressed his annoyance. "Look, we've got a problem here."

*She* had a problem. A sick baby. "I wouldn't take off if it wasn't necessary. You've worked with me long enough to know that."

"Six months ago, I would have agreed, but you've changed. Your production has decreased, you're missing work when we need you most and, frankly, I need someone I can depend on."

The words were clipped and sharp as though he'd been storing them up, prepared to unleash the volley at the right time. Apparently, this morning was the last straw.

"A child can't help getting sick." She kept her tone even but her insides shook. "Other mothers have to deal with this."

"That's the point. They deal with it. Someone else looks after their sick kids while they work."

She didn't have anyone else. Even the day care wouldn't take Alex with a fever.

"I'm still making the adjustment to motherhood, Shane. Cut me some slack. In time conditions should improve."

"We don't have time. We're on deadline."

He was being especially difficult this morning. She was tempted to ask if he'd had his coffee yet. "I'll work late tomorrow."

"I need you here today." The frosty tone was unrelenting.

"I understand that. I wish things were different but I can't come in." She disliked missing work, but what else could she do? Alex had to come first. "I'm sorry."

"So am I, Cassidy. This is a business. We have deadlines and clients who expect top-of-the-line, on-time work. If you can't do your job, perhaps I should look for someone who can."

Cassidy stiffened, incredulous. "Are you threatening to fire me?"

His huff of frustration grated on her nerves. "I'm stating facts. You have choices to make. Come to work or don't. Keep your job or don't. Your choice."

The threat scraped through her like nails on a chalkboard. Decide between a sick, orphaned baby and her job? What kind of choice was that?

Three months ago, the decision would have been swift and easy. She would have done anything to feather her career cap. This morning with her arms still achy and damp from holding Alex's hot, fussy body, she had to do what was right and best for him, regardless of the consequences.

Suddenly, the job wasn't so important, the drive to the top less enchanting.

"You know what, Shane? You're right. I have a choice to make." Drawing in a deep, quivering breath and praying like mad, she jumped into the abyss. "I choose Alex."

"Don't be stupid, Cassidy. I'm not asking you to give up the child."

"No, but you're asking me to choose work over a sick baby. I won't do that. Now, if you'll excuse me, I have a pediatrician to visit. And you have a position to fill."

With a trembling hand, she hung up the phone and blew out a long, shaky breath. Now she'd done it. She was jobless. She not only would never climb to the top of her game, she had jumped off the middle rung and removed the ladder.

Her grandmother would have a fit.

Tears pushed at the back of her eyelids. She blinked them away. The decision was made and she'd worry about the results later. Right now, her nephew was burning with fever, his eyes glassy and bright, and she was the only one around to help him.

That was far more important than designing a logo for a chain of restaurants.

By the time she'd changed and fed Alex, who ate little, the worst of the thunderstorm had passed and a steady shower of rain washed the morning. Cassidy debated on carrying an umbrella but between Alex, his diaper bag and her purse, she had no hands left. Making sure Alex was covered, Cassidy backed out of her apartment for the mad dash to the parking lot.

The smell of rain on warm concrete mixed with the exhaust fumes of passing cars. Cold rain pelted her from above, prickling the skin on her arms. Her hurried steps splattered droplets onto her pants legs.

As she bent forward to place Alex in his car seat, water dripped from the car roof down the back of her shirt. Gasping at the sudden cold, she shivered.

Footsteps sounded to her left. Then something popped at her back. Though she could only see his navy pant legs and gleaming black shoes speckled with water, Cassidy knew her visitor was Nic, still dressed in work uniform.

And he was holding an umbrella.

"Taking your shower outside this morning?" The baritone voice was amused.

"Don't be funny. I'm having a lousy day." She snapped Alex into his carrier, covered him with a light blanket and touched his forehead once more. The fever still burned.

As she straightened, her side bumped Nic's solid torso. The morning air was chilled, but he exuded a welcome warmth. Cassidy relented. Regardless of her reaction, she was relieved to see him.

"Sorry. Thanks for coming out with the umbrella. I thought you'd be asleep already."

His shift ended at seven and it was now eight-thirty.

"I was about to come up to your place. I saw your car in the lot and figured something must be wrong if you didn't go to work."

The words brought back the too-recent confrontation with her boss. Or rather, her former boss.

Oh dear, she really had quit her job. She closed her eyes for a second. When she opened them again, Nic had moved closer, eyebrows drawn together as he studied her face.

They were standing next to her car crowded beneath a black umbrella, so close she could see the night's scruffy growth of beard along his upper lip and feel the rise and fall of his breathing. Rain patted the concrete outside their intimate circle. The memory of their shared kiss trembled in the morning. Cars on the street swished passed. Water pooled along the street's edges sprayed in an arc behind their tires.

She was tired of handling everything alone and Nic was so wonderfully available. Cassidy resisted the urge to lean into him.

Almost tenderly, Nic rubbed his free hand down her chilled arm and then held on to her wrist. Just that small gesture, that single touch of his warm skin, comforted her.

"I see that look," he said, his brown eyes deepening to velvet espresso. "What's wrong?"

"Everything," Cassidy admitted, biting her lip to hold back the tears. "Most importantly, Alex is sick."

Nic's pose changed. He tensed and leaned around her to gaze through the car window at the dozing baby. "With what?"

"Fever. I can't get his temperature down, and he's fussy and won't take his bottle."

"Are you headed for the hospital?"

"Pediatrician's office."

He reached around her and opened the passenger door. "Get in. I'll drive."

"Nic, you don't have to do that." But she really could use the moral support. "You worked all night. You need to sleep."

With a cocky grin he said, "You know what I say about sleep."

Yes, she knew. He could sleep when he was dead. A shiver went through her that had nothing to do with the chilly dampness.

"You're cold. Get in." Still protecting her from the rain with the umbrella, Nic gave her a gentle shove. She went down without a fight. He leaned in and kissed her forehead. "Buckle up."

Bemused and too tired and concerned to argue with a man who would win anyway, Cassidy snapped her safety belt while Nic jogged around the car and climbed into the driver's seat. Holding the umbrella outside, he gave the handle a shake, popped it closed and tossed it into the backseat with a flourish.

As he cranked the car engine, Cassidy made one more feeble attempt. "You really don't have to go with me."

He didn't have to kiss her on the forehead, either. She was still contemplating that.

"Humor me. Alex is my little buddy. I need to."

She needed him, too, a fact that was becoming uncomfortably clear. In that moment with rain sluicing off the windshield and her life in a mess, Cassidy looked across at the man easing her Camry out of the parking lot and forgot all about Nic's occupation, forgot about his reputation and saw him for who he was.

And knew she loved him.

Notorious Nic, who owned more hearts than Alex had diapers, had stolen yet another—hers.

Nic sat beside Cassidy on pale-purple upholstered chairs in the surprisingly quiet and tidy waiting room of Dr. Margaret Fisher, waiting for Alex's name to be called. His stomach hollow and eyes gritty from lack of sleep, he wondered what he was doing here. Even the guys at the station had noticed his preoccupation with his neighbor and her new son. But one look at Cassidy and Alex through his front window this morning and he'd had no choice. They drew him with more power than an electromagnet.

Half a dozen other parents, mostly women, alternately wrestled small children and murmured reassurances. At a child-size table, two toddlers played with brightly colored toys and made car noises. Occasionally, a nurse appeared through a door to the left and all eyes turned in her direction as she called the next patient.

Alex was awake again, whimpering, his chubby face flushed. Nic's gut twisted at the sight of the little dude in discomfort.

"Want me to hold him awhile?"

Cassidy shook her head to decline, as he knew she would, but Nic took Alex anyway and laid the unresisting child lengthwise along his thighs. Alex's usual happy smile and vibrant energy were nowhere to be seen today.

"What do you suppose is wrong?" Cassidy murmured, her cornflower-blue eyes worried.

He lifted a shoulder. "We'll find out. Stop worrying. Babies get sick. They get well."

"Oh, great and wise baby expert." At least he'd roused a smile. "I visited your mother yesterday."

"Yeah?" That made him happy. He reached for her hand, happier still when she didn't resist. "How was she?"

"Strong as usual and ready to get the surgery over with."

The idea of his mother going under the knife shook him. "I scheduled Friday off duty to be there."

For some reason, he'd feel better if Cassidy was there, too, but he wouldn't ask. She had missed enough work already. He knew how much that bothered her, how important her career was.

"Do you mind if I come with you?" she asked, surprising him.

"Don't you have work that day?"

"No." Her chest rose and fell in a deep sigh. "I don't. This morning I joined the ranks of the unemployed."

He blinked at her, stunned. "Whoa, what happened?"

"My boss pressured me to come in to the office today and threatened to fire me if I didn't, so I quit."

"I thought your career was everything."

"Was." She stroked her index finger down Alex's cheek, the look in her eyes so full of love Nic's chest tightened with emotion. "Not anymore."

"What are you going to do?"

"I'll find something. Right now, we're fine. Janna and Brad had insurance. Alex and I inherited their estate. I'd intended to save the money for Alex's future so hopefully I can find work soon."

The nurse appeared at the door, holding a chart. Cassidy glanced her way but the name called wasn't Alex's.

"Won't you have the same problem with any company?" he asked. "I mean, with Alex."

He didn't add that she was overprotective, which could cause an issue with any boss. But she was still getting her parenting legs under her. The company should have been more understanding.

"Probably, but I'm sure something will work out. God didn't bring Alex and me this far to let us fall on our faces." She pressed a hand to Alex's cheek. Nic noticed her acrylic nails were missing. "We're a family now. We'll manage."

For all her brave talk, Cassidy was worried. Nic saw the truth in her troubled eyes, in the tightness around her mouth. She loved graphic design. She even created Web sites and other designs for friends simply because she loved the work.

An idea jiggled his consciousness. "Why not start your own business?"

She shook her head, blond hair whispering against her shoulders, but Nic saw a light go on behind her eyes.

He pressed. "Don't discard the idea too fast. You could work at home and take care of Alex without day care."

"Oh, that sounds good. Even the day care would love the idea. I drive them crazy calling every hour."

"You already have the contacts. You have the skills." He squeezed her fingers. "And you have a computer."

"I never thought I'd say this, Nic, but you're a good influence."

He laughed. She could say the cutest things. "And don't you forget it, either." Taking care not to disturb Alex, he leaned close to her ear and murmured, "Now, if I can only get you to come down and look at my etchings."

She patted the top of his head and gave it a little push. "I never did know what those were."

"Me, either," he admitted with a grin. "But I still want to show them to you."

The nurse appeared again and this time Alex was called.

Feeling more domestic than he thought possible, Nic gently brought Alex to his shoulder and followed Cassidy and the nurse down a short hall lined with posters. A few depicted scenes of child development or calls for immunization. One was a poster about an upcoming blood drive. Yet another announced a Run for the Cure, a race to raise money for breast cancer research. That was something he and his siblings could sink their teeth into.

*Lord, if a cure is possible, bring it on.*

He could hardly believe how much he'd prayed since his mother went into the hospital. Something had changed inside of him, something that felt good and right. God was the answer, whether he knew all the questions or not. Funny how it took something bad to bring him around to the goodness of God.

"This way, please. Room three." The curly-haired nurse smiled and showed them into a room. Nic dragged his eyes away from the pink-ribboned poster and went inside.

He and Cassidy sat side by side in hard, straight-backed chairs, their knees touching. Nic couldn't help himself. Even with Alex snuggled against his shoulder he pulled Cassidy's hand into his.

The nurse asked a bunch of questions, jotted notes and took Alex's vital signs. Then she patted the paper-lined cradle of a scale.

"If Daddy will just lay the baby in here for a minute."

Cassidy's startled gaze flew to his. She flushed. Nic's heart did a strange lurch that slammed into his rib cage before settling again.

"He's not—I mean, we're not—" Cassidy stuttered, getting nowhere.

Nic winked at her and rose to do the nurse's bidding. The woman's mistake was a natural one. No use getting embarrassed.

Especially since the idea of being Alex's dad didn't bother him all that much. He was nuts about the little dude. Since meeting Alex and Cassidy, a strange kind of yearning had moved in with him. Watching his brothers and sisters with their families increased the urge.

Beside him, Cassidy patted Alex in reassurance. She brushed against Nic's side, a beautiful, motherly princess, a woman of faith and strength that occupied his every waking thought. And sometimes his sleeping ones.

A new reality punched him in the gut. One that he wasn't ready for.

He might be nuts about Cassidy, too.

The idea shook him more than a five-alarm fire in a fifty-story building.

# Chapter Twelve

"Are you sure this isn't too much for you?"

Nic knelt on one knee next to a blue-striped lawn chair stationed on the sidewalk parallel to Broadway Avenue, the official start and finish line of the Run for the Cure. His mother, dressed in a pink shirt and cap, although she claimed the color did nothing for her, had insisted on watching the race even though she was still recovering from surgery.

"Don't worry, son." The aluminum legs of his dad's lawn chair clattered as he unfolded it next to Rosalie's. Other members of the Carano clan formed a watchful semicircle around Mom. "With all of us here, your mama doesn't stand a chance. One tired look and she's going home."

Rosalie patted her husband's weathered hand, a simple gesture Nic had seen hundreds of times over the years. Now, the depth and strength of their love and care for each other brought a lump to his throat. He saw the importance of what they shared...and wanted that same thing in his own life someday.

Of its own volition, his mind shot straight to Cassidy. He gazed around at the hoard of people crowding the streets and lining the race route, but didn't see her. She was here somewhere, preparing for the race. Earlier she'd dropped Alex off with Mia who had stayed home to look after the little ones. Although the little dude had recovered from his viral infection, Cassidy hadn't wanted to bring him out into a crowd, especially when she would be racing.

He spotted his sister's husband, Collin, dressed in police uniform as part of security. Seeing him reminded Nic of his own job here as one of many volunteer paramedics.

"I'm on my cell if you need me." He patted the instrument at his waist as he pushed to his feet.

"Those runners will need you more," his mother said.

"Yeah," Adam piped up from his spot just behind Mama. "Keep an eye on that pretty blond girl especially. You know the one. Big blue eyes. Dynamite smile. Looks great in running shorts."

He jabbed an elbow into his brother Gabe who added his two cents. "I heard she has a thing for firefighters."

Nic laughed off the teasing comments, waving as he headed for his assigned station.

The brothers were wrong. Cassidy didn't have a thing for firefighters. She might like him but she didn't like his profession. She'd told him as much.

He liked her, too. Good thing he wasn't going to be a fireman forever. He turned the situation over in his mind, thinking about exactly where he wanted the relationship to go. He didn't quite know yet, but he wanted to find out.

He wove his way through the spectators, thinking. His MCAT results would be back soon. With all the hard work he'd put in, he felt good this time about his chances for a top score. Yet, whenever he thought about the future, about leaving the fire department, his stomach tied into a hundred knots.

"Nic! Nic!"

Tottering on heeled sandals that Nic found ridiculous given

the outdoor sporting event, several girls of his acquaintance rushed toward him. He was outside a small tent near the finish line, administering first aid to those runners with cramps, dehydration and plain old fatigue. Most of the entrants were holding up well today in this relatively short race.

He smiled at the girls, but his usual zip was missing. He had an eye on the race and was waiting for Cassidy to come into sight.

"What's up, ladies?" he asked. "Why aren't you running for the cure?"

Mandy made a face. "And get all sweaty? No thanks."

"But we donated to the cause, Nic," Lacey hurried to add.

"I appreciate that." When word of his mother's cancer diagnosis spread, most of his friends had bonded together to either form running teams or to raise money. The gestures blessed him.

Mandy fanned her face with one hand, blocking his view. "Hot out here."

Nic stretched around her to watch the race. Where was Cassidy? He'd expected her to be in with the early finishers.

"Earth to Nic. Hello."

He refocused on the speaker. "What?"

"Got any cold drinks in that tent? I'm parched."

"Only for the runners."

"Well, pooh." Mandy pushed her bangs back. "A bunch of us are going to the dance and fireworks after the awards ceremony. Want to come along?"

Before she finished, he was already shaking his head. "Can't. But thanks for asking."

"Why not? You never want to do anything fun anymore." She pulled a pretty pout that would have worked on him in the past. He didn't understand why it didn't now, but it didn't. "What's the deal?"

Just then, he spotted a shiny platinum blond ponytail bobbing up and down in a group of about six runners. His heart lurched. Cassidy. Finally.

He reached for a bottle of water. She'd need this. His focus on that bounce of blonde, he stepped around his friends in order to better observe.

Cassidy broke loose from the pack. He could see her arms moving, still relaxed as she powered for the finish line. Man, she was something.

Rachel followed the direction of his gaze. "She's the one, isn't she?" Rachel accused, one hand to her hip in disbelief. "That blonde who lives upstairs from you. The one with the baby. She's the reason you never want to have fun anymore."

Cassidy, running at a steady pace, perspiration giving her face a glow, spotted him and smiled. When she saw the girls gathered around him, the smile faltered and she glanced away.

The action struck him as meaningful. Suddenly, he was feeling really good.

"Yes," he said, never taking his eyes off the race. "It's her."

Without further explanation, he moved away from the gaping girls and toward the oncoming runner.

As she crossed the finish line, he stepped into her path. Startled, she pulled up but stumbled, falling against him. Down they went onto the hard street. Nic could feel Cassidy's heart pounding wildly against her rib cage. She was damp with perspiration and her breath came in deep drags.

Cassidy pushed away and sat up, arms over her knees to draw in deep drafts of fresh air.

"Good race," Nic said.

She grinned into his eyes, breathing hard but not struggling. Nic felt the strongest need to kiss her. Instead, he handed her the water bottle.

She took the bottle gratefully, uncapped and gulped down

most of the contents. As she tilted back her head, Nic noticed her T-shirt. The same bright pink his mother wore, Cassidy's T-shirt displayed something special—a huge screen-printed photo of his mother with the words, "In honor of my hero, Rosalie Carano."

Nic's throat clogged with emotion. He draped an arm around the woman at his side and gently kissed her hair.

No doubt about it. If he hadn't been in love with Cassidy Willis before, he was now.

After the successful race Cassidy was stoked, so much so that she let Nic talk her into leaving Alex with Mia again that evening while they attended the race day finale, live entertainment and a dance. The idea of spending a romantic evening with Nic was both exhilarating and nerve-racking but she wouldn't have missed it for the world. In spite of her best intentions, she'd fallen in love with him.

"Your sister is a doll for babysitting Alex," she said as they entered the ballroom and started to weave their way through the crowd.

As a runner, she and her date were allotted a table close to the bandstand. Her date. Nic Carano. Her heart danced a happy jig. Would wonders never cease?

Somehow she'd convinced herself that once Nic left his dangerous job and entered medical school everything would be all right. The flock of females fluttering around him at the race should have stopped her in her tracks, but they hadn't.

Rosalie's words played in her head. If Nic wanted to be with those other girls, he would be. He'd chosen her, not only tonight but over and over again in recent weeks.

The reasonable portion of her brain said she was asking for a broken heart, and yet in the last few months she'd done a lot of unreasonable things. Just ask Grandmother.

"Can't argue that," Nic was saying, a hand at the small of her back as he guided her through the crush. "Mia's a jewel."

She turned her head to look at him, her stomach dipping at the look in his eyes. "We'll have to babysit for her and Collin some night and let them go out alone."

"Sounds good. You and me snuggled on the couch listening to romantic music while the rug rats play." They'd reached their table and Nic pulled out a chair, waiting for her to sit. As she did, he leaned down to nuzzle her hair, jump-starting her pulse.

Her heart as light as a helium balloon, she touched the side of his face, wishing she could hold him near this way forever. His clean, masculine smell lingered after he broke contact and took his own seat.

"If I know you," she said, not about to let him know how affected she was by his nearness, "you'll be on the floor playing with the rug rats."

"Mmm, maybe not. None of them smell as good as you." He scraped his chair closer and leaned in.

Cassidy smiled on the inside. Hadn't she just been thinking the same about him? "You couldn't have said that earlier today."

"Sure, I could have. It wouldn't have been true, but I could have said it."

She whacked his arm. "Flatterer."

"All for a good cause. When I saw your T-shirt—wow." His fisted hand thudded once against his chest. "Got me right there."

"Your mom's a special woman."

"Yeah." Some of his ebullience faded.

Hurting for him, Cassidy touched his arm. "She's going to beat the cancer, Nic. I believe that with all my heart."

His nostrils flared. "We're trying to stay optimistic."

"You're the king of optimism. That's one of the things I—" About to blurt that she loved him, Cassidy stopped the flow of words in the nick of time and fiddled with the small napkin under her soft drink.

Nic was different tonight. He felt much more like a date and far less like her goofy neighbor. But she wasn't complaining. She felt different, too, and had since he'd met her at the end of the race. Nonetheless, she had to be careful. Spilling her heart would be easy to do. A mistake perhaps, but easy.

Nic pushed a bowl of pretzels toward her. "Have I told you how pretty you look?"

She'd spent an inordinate amount of time trying to decide what to wear tonight, which was silly. Nic had seen her at her worst during the days of Alex's colic.

Finally, she'd settled on a white and turquoise polka-dot sundress with matching bracelets, a white belt that cinched her waist and white sandals. The expression on Nic's face when she'd opened her door told her she'd chosen well.

"You look pretty good yourself, mister." His snow-white polo shirt set off his dark skin and black hair to perfection.

They smiled into each other's eyes and Cassidy felt the effects of either runner's high or Nic Carano. Maybe both.

A five-piece band kicked off with a well-known country tune. They listened for a while, talking in between tunes and sipping cold sodas. Nic's lighthearted banter, his funny comments about the band, the music and the dancers relaxed them both. He was so easy to be with.

When the band eased into a slow song Nic leaned in, dark eyes mesmerizing. "Want to dance?"

She shook her head. "I'm not much of a dancer."

"That's okay." A grin played around his mouth. "Dancing's just an excuse to hold you anyway. No expertise required."

"You're silly."

"Serious. Come on." He scraped back his chair and stood, holding out a hand. "We'll stand on the dance floor and hold each other while the band plays. No one will know we don't dance."

His sense of the ridiculous never failed to get to her. He was joking, teasing, being his usual funny self. But she had to admit, the idea of being in Nic's arms sounded good.

Feeling almost giddy, Cassidy placed her palm against Nic's and let him lead her to the dance floor. Dozens of festivity-goers crowded the long, narrow ballroom, many of whom spoke to Nic as they passed. A mix and mingle of voices and cologne and music swirled around them, heady and rich.

Cassidy thought she should be tired after today's race, but she wasn't. She was exhilarated, partly because of her good race time and the successful fund-raiser, but more because of the man at her side.

Instead of joining the crowd as she'd expected him to do, Nic worked his way to the perimeter of the room. Any farther away and they'd be out on the wide porch.

"Here we go." He slid an arm around her waist, pulling her near but not so close as to breach respectability. She appreciated that.

They swayed in time to the music, talking most of the time, though Cassidy was acutely conscious of everywhere Nic touched her.

"Any new business ventures?" he asked, gazing down with the most enthralling, heart-stopping expression. What, she wondered, was he thinking?

"You're not going to believe this, but my grandmother sent some work my way. She actually likes the idea of me being my own boss."

"I'm shocked speechless."

Cassidy laughed. "You've never been speechless in your life."

"True." He cocked his head to one side. "Well, maybe once."

"When?" she asked in disbelief, sure he was still teasing.

By now, Nic had guided them smoothly out onto the porch and into the cooler evening air. The night pulsed around them; light flowed from the interior like butter melted across the concrete. Cars passed on the street and doors slammed; people came and went in nearby restaurants.

Nic's expression grew serious.

"The first time ever I saw your face," he said, quoting the old song.

Though the sentiment touched her, Cassidy refused to let him see. "Because I looked so awful?"

Instead of the witty rejoinder she expected, Nic's voice dropped low and Cassidy could see the pulse beating in the hollow of his throat.

"Not even close," he murmured, drawing her slowly nearer until they were heart to heart, his gaze holding hers with stunning intensity. Her own pulse fluttered, with the scariest, most amazing feeling she'd ever had.

"Why then?"

"Because," he said, dark eyes liquid with something she couldn't fully read. "You stopped me in my tracks."

Cassidy fought the surge of tenderness, fought the melting of her resistance. "You probably say that to all the girls."

"No," he said, voice laced with frustration. "I don't. Come on, Cass, throw me a bone here. I'm trying to be romantic."

"Am I crushing your ego?" she asked, more for self-preservation than to get an answer. She was sinking fast.

His jaw tightened. "Is that what you want? To crush my ego?"

Stunned to think she could, Cassidy was suddenly contrite. She touched a palm to his smooth-shaven jaw and echoed his words in a whisper, "Not even close."

The tension left his body as he exhaled a long breath and rested his face in her hair.

"Something's going on between us, Cass," he murmured, the words warm against her scalp. "Don't you feel it, too?"

Oh, yes, she felt it. As powerful and overwhelming as a tsunami. Throat filled with inexpressible emotion, she nodded.

Nic tilted her head, strong hands bracketing her face with such tenderness. His fingertips made soothing circles at her hairline, his handsome face so near she could see the rims of brown iris circling black pupils.

"I care for you, Cassidy. A lot."

"More than your entourage?"

"My what?"

"Mandy and Candy or whoever all those girls are." If she sounded like a jealous woman, so be it. She needed to know.

"Way more. More than any woman I've ever known."

His heart beat against hers and she could feel the *thud-thud* inside his chest. He was telling her the truth.

Gulping back the fear, Cassidy admitted, "I care for you, too, Nic. More than I can say."

As if he'd been uncertain of her response, Nic pressed his forehead to hers and sighed. Music filtered out from the dance and they swayed in time, oblivious to everything else around them.

"So what are we going to do about it?" he murmured, his warm lips brushing her hairline as he spoke.

The possibilities were both wonderful and fearful.

"I don't know," she whispered. They were moving toward something that would either bring heartache or joy. Did she dare to take the risk with a man like Nic?

He lifted his head to melt her with a look. "Me, either. But how about this for starters?"

His lips touched hers in a kiss so shatteringly sweet,

Cassidy forgot her reservations as she returned the gentle pressure. Only when a thin siren's wail broke above the other sounds, did she remember.

It required all her strength, all her resolve, to step away from Nic's embrace.

Nic reached for her, caught her arm and tugged. "Don't do that, Cassidy. Don't pull away out of fear."

"I can't help it, Nic. Please understand."

"I do understand. I know what you've been through. I know why fire terrifies you. After all the people you've lost, I'd be an idiot not to understand."

Desperately wanting things to be different and hating herself for spoiling their romantic evening, she stepped toward him. With the flat of her hand against his chest, she said, "Don't give up on me, Nic."

His arms went around her, drawing her back to him. Softly he said, "I couldn't if I wanted to."

Hope returned. Maybe, just maybe, she and Nic could make this work. Tiptoeing, she kissed the dimple in his chin. "Once you leave the fire department everything will be fine."

A muscle beneath his eye twitched. His gaze slid away to stare into the dark evening.

"Sure," he said finally. "Everything will be great."

But as Cassidy's cheek rested against the thudding of Nic's heart, she couldn't help wondering about that moment of hesitation.

# Chapter Thirteen

Cassidy hit the Send key on her computer and rolled back in the desk chair with a satisfied smile. One of Grandmother's business contacts had just accepted her bid for a full Web site redesign, mail-out brochures and a logo update.

She stretched her arms high over her head to release the tension in her shoulders. Old-time rock and roll issued from her computer speakers. She stood to jitterbug around Alex's playpen located next to her desk.

Life was good.

The thought caught her up short. She pulled it back like a curtain and considered it again. A few months ago, she could not have said such a thing.

"Thank you, sweet Lord," she murmured. God had been faithful. He'd given her strength to face Janna's death. He'd given her more joy than she ever imagined possible in Alex. Even when she'd lost her dream job, God had sent a better replacement.

Granted she wasn't making as much money yet, but she was far happier running her own business.

Nic Carano's idea had been positively inspired.

She smiled. Nic. Something really beautiful was growing there, too. She had even begun dreaming of a future with him once he left the fire department.

"Which makes both of us happy, doesn't it, lambkin?" Cassidy leaned over the playpen rail to caress Alex's sweet face. The baby had loved Nic first and had become the magnet that drew them together until fantasies of a real family played through her mind like a sweet melody. She, Nic and Alex.

Her baby nephew was such a precious boy. He deserved a mother *and* a father. Nic would be a wonderful father. She was certain of it. He loved this child, and though motherhood had changed her drastically, Cassidy was thrilled to be Alex's mommy.

She swept him into her arms.

"You are getting so big," she said. He cackled as if she'd said the funniest thing. Cassidy laughed, too, full of love for her nephew.

She sat Alex on the carpet and eased down in front of him to play. Lately she had to watch him every minute he was out of the playpen. He could roll from one side of the living room to the other faster than she could turn off a light switch. She'd discovered this the hard way one evening when she'd gone into the kitchen to snap off the light only to turn around and find him under her feet.

"Little stinker." She wiggled his favorite squeaky toy. "Come get your bunny."

Alex blew a sloppy, wet raspberry. Cassidy laughed, her mind drifting to Nic again. He and Alex exchanged raspberries on a daily basis. Nic's were normally administered to Alex's pudgy belly, an action that caused gales of delight from the baby.

From Cassidy, too. Watching Nic with Alex blessed her all the way to her bones.

Since the dance, they'd seen each other every day that

Nic wasn't on duty. Sometimes he jogged up the steps just to kiss her good-night. On those occasions she went to sleep with a smile.

Today, he'd spent the morning with his mother, but he'd invited her down to his place for lunch at noon. Cassidy glanced up at the sunburst clock. Soon.

She'd thought and thought about his odd reaction to her comment the night of the dance. Surely she must have imagined the doubt in his eyes.

*Lord, don't let me be wrong.*

Nic wanted to be a doctor. Med school was his dream. Now it was hers.

Once he resigned from the fire department she could breathe a sigh of relief, knowing he was safe. All her doubts and fears and anxieties would disappear then. They could be together without worry, without fear, without the deadly danger of losing someone else she loved.

Yes, as soon as he left firefighting, everything would be perfect.

At five minutes before noon, Cassidy swung happily down the stairs with Alex on her hip. She passed the postman and intercepted her mail, saving him a jog up to her apartment.

"Nothing but junk anyway," she said, not caring one iota.

The carrier probably heard the complaint on a daily basis because he only smiled and moved on down the sidewalk. The rise and fall of metal mailbox lids clanked in an irregular rhythm as he distributed his load.

Cassidy pounded on Nic's door as the carrier dropped several envelopes into the slot on the exterior wall.

Nic whipped the door open with a flourish.

"Soup's on," he declared, taking Alex from her grasp and giving her a peck on the nose during the exchange.

"Mail's here," she shot back, reaching under the lid to extract three envelopes and a sale insert. "Home Depot has chain saws on sale. Want one?"

"Don't tempt me. Every man wants a chain saw." He swung Alex in a circle. "Power tools rule."

"I'll remember that on your birthday."

He looked pleased.

"What else did I get? Bills?" he asked, indicating the mail in her hand.

She'd been so engrossed in looking at him with Alex and enjoying that rush of pleasure at the bond between them, her mind had strayed.

She turned the envelopes upright. "Looks like the electric bill, cable and—" she frowned down at the return address. "—I don't know what this one is."

"Let me see." Coming to her side, he leaned over her shoulder.

As if the sun had gone behind a cloud, his countenance changed. His smile faded. His stared at the envelope long enough for Cassidy to know something was wrong. Before she could ask, he took the missive from her fingertips, dropped it on the end table and headed for the kitchen.

"What is that, Nic?"

"Nothing much." But he didn't look at her.

"Then why are you acting so weird?"

"Is it okay if I put Alex on the floor while I dish up the grub?" he asked, clearly changing the subject. He knew she didn't mind if Alex played on the little mat. That's what it was there for. He even kept a basket of toys next to the couch.

Baffled by Nic's behavior, she picked up the troubling piece of mail and reread the return address. Realization crept in like a thief, stealing her pleasure. "These are your MCAT scores, aren't they?"

She stared at him across the divide of living and dining room. His reluctant expression terrified her.

"Nic?" What in the world was going through his head?

His chest rose and fell in a great huff of air. "Yeah, I think so."

"What's wrong?" She started toward him, heart thudding heavily. "Are you worried about the results?"

Surely that was it. Surely he was afraid of failing again.

"You could say that." But his gaze slid away from hers. "Put them over there. I'll look at them later."

"Nic, you passed. I know you did. You studied so hard. There's no way you didn't do well." She tapped his shoulder with the letter. "Come on, let's open this so we can celebrate."

"Leave it, Cassidy." He yanked the envelope from her hands.

Stung, she could only stare at him, reading the truth behind his behavior.

Instantly contrite, he reached for her hands and pulled her to him. "Hey, I'm sorry. Didn't mean to take a bite out of you."

"When were you going to tell me?"

He couldn't look her in the eyes. "Leave it alone, Cassidy. This is something I have to deal with."

"I thought you wanted to go to medical school," she said softly, longing for him to say he still did.

He pulled away to lean both hands against the divider bar. Head down, he said, "I thought so, too."

"But you changed your mind?"

A long beat passed while she waited for an answer. Alex slammed a toy against the floor. Cars roared past on the street. And Cassidy's heart broke.

"I know how much this means to you, Cassidy."

Did he? Did he have any idea of the terror she felt every time he went to work? Did he know of the hopes and dreams she'd let seep into a guarded heart that knew the dangers of loving?

"You don't want to leave the fire department," she mumbled, almost to herself. One of them had to speak the words.

"I thought I could. I wanted to. For you. For my family…"

His voice drifted away on a tide of bewildered sadness.

"But it's not what you want." Tears gathered, threatening. "Is it?"

*Please say I'm mistaken. Please say this is one of your silly jokes.*

But she knew he was telling the truth. He had tried to be something he wasn't for her and his family. In the process, he'd lied to them all, even himself.

"I'm sorry, Cass."

"So am I, Nic. More sorry than I can ever say." Sorry that there could be no future for them now.

"This doesn't change us," he said, pushing off the counter, his palms upright, beseeching. "We can work this out."

As much as she longed to fall into his arms, Cassidy backed away, heart shattering like glass on tile. "There's nothing to work out, Nic. I can't ask you to give up the work you love any more than you can ask me to give up Alex."

She bent to gather the baby into her arms. Lunch held no appeal for her now.

"I'd never do that."

"Exactly. I won't ask you to give up your career. But I can't be a part of it, either. I can't live like that, in constant fear for your safety, terrified every time you leave the house that you won't come back. I can't. Please understand," she pleaded. "I can't take a chance on losing anyone else."

She had started to shake, afraid of letting him go but more afraid of staying.

He noticed and moved toward her. She held out a hand, freezing him in his tracks. If he touched her, if he held her, she might crumble, and then this scene would have to play again. Because she couldn't, wouldn't, take this kind of chance. She and Alex needed a man who would always be there for them. They couldn't bear another loss.

"So where do we go from here?" he asked quietly.

Back to being alone. Back to struggling through each day, hoping the next will be better. Back to safety.

But she only said, "I'm sorry, Nic."

So terribly, brokenly sorry. So sorry that if she didn't leave now she would fall into a heap and beg to stay.

His throat worked as her words soaked in. "So this is it, huh? Goodbye, adios, farewell?"

She could read the hurt and bewilderment in his eyes, see that he felt betrayed.

In that moment, she hated herself as much as she hated the tragedies that had taken her family.

With all the self-preserving strength she could muster, she reached back to open the door. Her fingers trembled against the cold knob. She gripped it hard, holding on.

"I think that's best." The words rasped from her tight, aching throat.

Face like flint, Nic nodded.

Alex reached for him and the stony expression cracked. With a tenderness that nearly killed her, Nic kissed Alex's outstretched fingers and then touched her cheek. She fought not to close her eyes and lean into him. Instead, she kept her gaze trained on Alex. Looking at Nic would destroy her.

"I'm sorry, Nic," she whispered.

"So am I, Cass. So am I."

Blinded by a swarm of tears pushing to break free, she whirled away and rushed toward the steps leading to her apartment.

Breaking things off now was for the best. Wasn't it?

But as she stumbled into her living room, the sobs came and didn't stop for the longest time.

\* \* \*

Nic kicked the door shut and stood, hands on hips, staring at the white paint. His knees trembled and his mouth was drier than the Sahara. A knot the size of Philadelphia rested just beneath his breastbone.

Stupid. He was stupid to have ever gotten involved with Cassidy in the first place. But he couldn't leave well enough alone. He'd pushed and charmed and forced his way into her life. She hadn't wanted him from the start. Why hadn't he gotten the message?

Her fire phobia should have been a red alert.

Dumb Nic thought he could cure her, thought if she loved him she would trust him, and the fear would go away.

"So much for the knight in shining turnout gear." The words meant to be sarcastic burned in his mouth as bitter as gall.

He kicked the leg of the couch. Pain shot up his foot, grimly satisfying and far less painful than a massacred heart.

He flopped into his recliner. Something shoved into his back. He reached around and withdrew a teddy bear. The anger went out of him like air from a punctured tire. He pressed the plush toy to his lips.

"I love her," he said to the sweet-faced bear. "I know you didn't think it was possible for a guy like me to get serious about one girl. I didn't, either. But there you have it. I love her. I thought she felt the same. Dumb, huh?"

The teddy bear stared back at him with shiny black eyes and a red smile. Nic pressed the toy to his chest in much the same way he sometimes held Alex.

For the longest time he sat there, clutching the bear, wishing he could be what others needed him to be and wondering how he was going to laugh his way through this.

The painful truth ripped at his insides. He couldn't. Getting over Cassidy and Alex was going to take a lot more than that.

With a heart heavier than a fire engine, he tossed the teddy bear into the basket next to his couch. As soon as the toy landed he got up and retrieved it, holding it on his lap as he'd done with Alex.

"Me and you, buddy," he said, a depressing statement that got him thinking.

He needed friends and fun around him. That was the only cure he knew for the blues. If Cassidy didn't want him, there were those who did, regardless of his career choice. He pulled out his cell phone and dialed.

By nightfall his apartment was rocking, packed with as many friends as he could round up on short notice. They crowded every room, talking, playing video games and jiving around to the music pumping from his stereo.

Slim Jim and Ty, another of his firefighter buddies, manned the grill, scorching burgers and dogs for the gang. Rachel, Mandy, Lacey and his other lady friends handed out chips and drinks, flirting with and teasing every guy in the place. Laughter abounded. Party Central was in full swing. Everyone was having a blast.

Everyone but the host.

"Great party, Nic." Someone slapped him on the shoulder.

"Thanks." He tried to smile but the action was too much work. Excusing himself, he rotated through the rooms, hoping something would snap him out of his lousy mood.

Instead, the revelry only depressed him more.

After an hour of forcing smiles he didn't feel and telling jokes that annoyed him, Nic grabbed a Coke from an ice chest and escaped outside. He stood on the sidewalk for a minute before venturing over to the stairs leading up to Cassidy's apartment. He stared up at the closed door. She was in there. She had to know he was having a party. She probably thought he was down here having the time of his life.

With a heavy sigh, Nic sat on the bottom step and sipped his soda. The carbonated fizz burned his throat, adding to the hot ache in his chest. Few things got him down. He was the life of the party, the fun guy.

Tonight he was dying. And he didn't even care. The party held no charm for him. Here in the dark with cars zipping past and music floating out of his apartment, he felt more alone than he could remember. And it was his own fault.

He should have told Cassidy from the start that he didn't want to leave the fire department. But he hadn't known for sure until the day he'd taken the MCAT. As he'd answered question after question with surprising knowledge and insight, he'd known he was doing well. Instead of triumph, his gut had knotted with dread.

When he'd begun praying about the choice, the dread got worse.

Maybe he should go ahead with the plan anyway and become a doctor. Then everyone would be happy. His family, Cassidy, everyone. Except him.

"You're messed up, dude," he said to the darkness. Messed up because he loved a woman he couldn't have and remain true to himself. Messed up because he wanted to make his parents proud, especially now that Mama was sick. She needed to know her baby boy was going to be something besides a goof-off.

He stared up into the night sky, wishing he could see the stars, but knowing they were obliterated by the city lights. God was up there somewhere. He was here, too, according to everything Nic believed, though tonight God felt far away.

"I could use some advice, Lord," he murmured.

He downed the rest of the cola and crushed the empty can in one hand. After a minute, he rose, balanced the crooked can on a window ledge and then jogged toward the parking lot.

* * *

"You love her." His mother's words were a statement of fact, not a question. As always, Mama had suspected the truth, probably before he had.

"Yeah." The admission was a lead weight.

Like he'd done as a boy when trouble came, Nic sat at the table in his parents' terra-cotta kitchen, surrounded by the familiar trappings of his family. See-through jars of pasta lined the counter. Copper pots hung over the center island, shiny in the artificial light. The smell of chocolate chip cookies, warm from the oven, and freshly perked coffee filled the place.

When he'd asked God for advice, this had been his answer. Just being here gave him hope that he'd get through this in one piece.

His mother and dad sat together, a united force as they'd always been, facing him. The dark circles beneath Mama's eyes made him feel a little guilty.

"Maybe I shouldn't have come. Mom's not up to this." He started to rise.

"Sit." Dad didn't say a lot, but he meant what he said. "Tell us what happened."

Nic sat and let the words tumble out. When he got to the part about retaking the MCAT, his mother gasped. "And you didn't tell us? Oh, Nicky, why?"

Before Nic could answer, his father spoke. "Rosalie, listen to what the boy is not saying."

With a quizzical expression his mother studied his father and then him. She nodded. "I see. Yes, I see. You didn't fail this time, but you're not happy about it."

More miserable than he could say, he dropped his face into his hands. "I don't know what to do."

"What do you want?"

There was the million-dollar question. "I want the people

I love to be happy, but I can't be something I'm not. I thought I could, for you, for Cassidy—"

His mother placed a soft hand over his. "Stop. Look at me, Nic, and listen good."

Nic raised his face and saw the deep love glimmering in her Sicilian eyes.

"God gave you a special gift. You bring joy just by being alive. When you arrive, the room lights up, people laugh and feel happy."

"Nothing special about being a goof-off."

"You see it as a goof-off, but we know better." She patted him. "Oh, don't misunderstand, we've had our concerns, but no more with you than with the other children. We've watched you struggle and grow and come out stronger. Under that handsome smile is the heart of a lion. Your dad and I are proud of the man you've become."

Unaccustomed moisture sprang to Nic's eyes. His parents thought that? He looked at his father and saw his mother's remarks echoed there. "But Gabe and Adam are lawyers. I thought—" He shook his head. "I don't know. That being a doctor would make us even."

"We're proud of your brothers, but what you do is just as important. Law and medicine are noble careers, but so is firefighting. If not for you, baby Alex would never have made it into the hands of a physician. You saved him first."

He'd never looked at it that way.

"So you aren't going to disown me if I withdraw my medical school application?" he asked, only half joking.

His dad pushed the plate of cookies toward him. "My father was a baker and his father before him was a baker. I chose to be a baker, too, not because Papa expected it, but because I wanted to. I like the smell of yeast and the feel of the dough. I like making people smile with an extra donut in the bag. I'm a happy man, fulfilling the destiny God gave me. All I ever wanted for my children was the same—to be fulfilled and content in their lives. You don't have to be a baker or a doctor or a lawyer. You just have to be Nic, the man God intended you to be." Leo sat back and breathed in through his nose, his barrel chest expanding. "And I will be proud."

The speech was one of the longest he'd ever heard from his father. Nic took a cookie, thinking of the love his parents put into everything they baked at Carano's Bakery. He understood that kind of passion because he felt it every time he donned his uniform.

A weight seemed to lift from his shoulders.

"Thanks, Dad. Mom." He bit into the buttery cookie and savored the semisweet chocolate on his tongue, but savored more the knowledge that his family was behind him. "You always know what to say."

"What about your relationship with Cassidy?"

His mother's gentle question plummeted him back into the depths of despair.

"Unless I leave the fire department, there is no relationship."

"Your career is your calling. Turning your back on your life's work is not the answer to Cassidy's problem." Rosalie reached for the coffeepot, but Leo beat her to it. "Does she love you?"

"I thought so. Apparently not enough."

"I saw her looking at you the way Mama looks at me." Pouring more coffee into each cup, Leo winked at Rosalie, who winked back. "She loves you. But fear rules her life."

"She has reason to be afraid, Dad." He'd told them about the tragedy in the Philippines. "She was buried alive, her parents dead, smoke circling like a vulture. Now her sister's dead."

Rosalie spooned creamer into her cup and stirred but didn't drink. "These are all tragic circumstances, but the Lord never intended any of us to be a slave to fear."

"There's nothing I can do to change her mind, Mom. The decision is hers."

His mother got a look on her face that he'd seen dozens of times. He and his siblings called it the mother tiger look—protective, determined and full of fierce love.

"There *is* something we can do." She extended an up-turned palm to each side, capturing his hand and his father's. "Let's pray."

# Chapter Fourteen

Nic drove around for a while after leaving his parents' house. Sometimes he prayed. Sometimes he just drove and thought about what a great family he had. He was blessed beyond anything he deserved. Thankfully he'd wised up.

He'd wised up about a couple of other things, too. If he loved Cassidy the way his dad loved his mother, he wouldn't sit around moping. He would take action.

But his ego still smarted from her rejection. If she loved him, she'd try harder to overcome her fears.

The dilemma warred inside him like two gladiators, each as strong as the other.

The night was warm and humid. He kicked on the AC and then the CD player. Worship music flowed out.

The CD was Cassidy's. She must have forgotten it the night of the race.

Considering the CD as good an excuse as any, he turned his truck toward the apartment complex where he parked in a no-parking zone directly beneath the steps leading to Cassidy's apartment.

From his own home came the sounds of the party in progress. In the shadowy darkness, he made a wry face. His friends hadn't even missed him. He rubbed his chest with the flat of his hand. Today was an ego-crushing day and the ego at risk was his.

He took the CD, jogged up the steps and pounded on Cassidy's door. From inside he heard the television playing. Someone laughed. She was having a good time without him. His ego took another nosedive. Here he was moping and she wasn't.

Nic fidgeted, waiting only a few seconds before pounding again. If she didn't open the door quick, he might chicken out.

The door swung open. Backlit by pale lamplight, Cassidy looked as pretty as an angel, her hair glowing gold. Nic swallowed, more nervous than he could remember.

"Hey," he said.

"Nic."

"You forgot this." He held out the CD.

She took it. "Thanks."

He was hoping she'd invite him in. She didn't.

Okay, why had he come up here? To make a fool of himself?

"I thought you might want it back."

"I appreciate it."

"The music's good."

"I like it."

Talk about a sparkling conversation. This was not one.

Behind her, voices murmured. Nic's defenses rose. Was she with another guy?

A female voice called, "Cassidy, who's out there?"

His shoulders relaxed the tiniest bit.

Cassidy called over her shoulder. "It's Nic."

As she turned her head, the light illuminated her face. Nic saw what he hadn't seen in the shadow. Puffy, swollen eyes were redder than her nose. She'd been crying.

His heart dropped to the toes of his Nikes. Okay, that was it. No crying on his shift.

He grabbed her hand. "We need to talk. Let's take a drive."

She shook her head, pulling away. Pale hair swished softly against the shoulders of a shiny blue blouse. "I can't. I have company."

At that moment, two teenage girls appeared at her side. He recognized them from her Bible Study.

"We're not company," one of them said, eyeing Nic with interest. "Go."

Apparently, they'd overheard his invitation.

Still Cassidy hesitated, but something in the way she looked at him said she wanted to go.

"Come on, Cass. Just for a while. We need to talk."

"Talking won't do any good, Nic. Besides Alex is already in bed for the night."

Nic's hopes fell.

One of the girls gave Cassidy's back a little push. "Go on, Cassidy. Katie and I will watch Alex."

Nic held his breath while the love of his life teetered on the edge. Finally, when he was at the point of light-headedness, she capitulated.

Though her expression was grim and hopeless, she said, "Let me get my shoes."

Cassidy sat against the passenger door wondering why she'd agreed to this ride with Nic. Being this close to him again was nothing but torture.

"Aren't you missing your own party?" The question was almost an accusation. She'd seen the trail of people roaming in and out of the parking lot and heard the gaiety from below. The notion that he could throw a party only hours after their breakup hurt. For all his declarations of caring for her, the party spoke volumes about his sincerity.

He made a smooth turn onto the main highway. "I missed what wasn't there."

"Meaning what? Mandy or Brandy or Candy didn't show up?" She sounded every bit like a jealous woman. She shouldn't have come with him tonight, not while she was still so emotional. She was the one who couldn't move forward. She was the one who was stuck in fear. Why should she be upset if Nic wanted to move on with his life as soon as possible?

Because she loved him, that was why.

As they pulled into heavier traffic, he glanced her way. The dash lights cast him in gray shadow with only the focal points of his bone structure clear. Except for the dark coal of vividly alive eyes, he was like a sculpture, perfectly cast.

He never bothered to counter her foolish questions. Instead his words touched her to the core. "You've been crying."

She crossed her arms against a rush of longing to be in his arms again. "Is that what you wanted to talk about?"

"I want to discuss anything that makes you unhappy."

"Don't do this, Nic. Caring about each other is not enough. I know you care for me and Alex." Her voice choked. "We care for you, too."

"What about love? Is love enough?"

Was he saying he loved her? Even if he did, what good was it under the circumstances?

She closed her eyes against the rush of hopelessness. "Love can't enter into the equation. In some weird way, I feel that if I don't love you, I'm protecting you. People I love die."

"That's not rational, sweetheart." The baritone was gentle, but she heard his frustration. "You have to know that."

"Of course I know," she moaned, desperate for him to understand. This was for his good as well as her own. "But I can't help my feelings. Wonderful people I love die. That's a fact. You work in a dangerous profession. Your life is in jeopardy every time you go to work. I can't live with that kind of worry, Nic. I can't."

He was silent for a few seconds, attention focused on the road and traffic. An eighteen-wheeler passed, lights bright and blinding. Nic's truck wobbled in the powerful wake.

A sigh as soft as Alex's breath escaped him. Cassidy felt his heaviness and ached for all the things she couldn't change.

"We're praying for you," he said quietly. "That's the main thing I wanted to tell you. Mom, Dad, me. I went to their house tonight. We prayed together. We'll keep praying."

The revelation moved her to tears.

Cassidy pressed a hand to her forehead. What was wrong with her? She had faith for so many things. Why couldn't she have faith to conquer this?

Somewhere she'd heard that fear was the opposite of faith. The statement had hurt her terribly. She wanted to have more faith. She just didn't know how to get it.

"Take me home, Nic. This is only making things worse."

By now, they'd driven to the outskirts of town where the traffic thinned and a few stars could be seen above the city lights. Nic's shoulders slumped and she knew she'd hurt him yet again. She hated herself and wished a thousand times she'd followed her instincts the first time they'd met and stayed away.

But this man wasn't the Notorious Nic she'd wanted to avoid. This man was solid and strong and caring, and far more dangerous to her heart.

Without argument, Nic hit the signal light and turned, taking the side streets back to the apartment.

They'd driven several blocks, through one quiet neighborhood and into another when a frighteningly familiar scent invaded Cassidy's nostrils.

"Nic."

He glanced her way, eyes wary. "Yeah?"

"Do you smell that?" The blood began to pound in her temples. "It's smoke, Nic. I smell smoke."

The words were barely out of her mouth when Nic slammed on the brakes.

"There," he said. "That house."

The dash lights reflected off Nic's face, painting him yellow and red—the colors of fire. Slowly, she turned her head, mesmerized by the smoke billowing from one side of a sprawling brick house.

"Call 9-1-1." He popped the latch on his seat belt, reaching for the door handle at the same time.

Cassidy grabbed his arm. "What are you doing?"

"There may be people inside."

The knowledge of what he was about to do slammed into her with the force of a freight train. Rising panic clogged her lungs.

"No!" The scream was ripped from somewhere deep inside. She clawed at him. "You can't."

He placed a hand over hers, a light touch of reassurance.

Gently but firmly, he said, "I have to be sure no one is in there. Don't worry. It's only smoke."

She was not reassured. Flames could burst forth at any moment.

Frantically, she clung, desperate to hold him back. "No. I won't let you. Something bad will happen."

In a rush now, he peeled her fingers away. "What if that was Alex in there?"

What could she say to that? Stricken and terrified, her hands fell uselessly to her sides. Nic slid from the truck, his mind already leaving her behind as he focused on the burning house.

"Promise me you won't do anything stupid," she begged. "Promise me."

He had already moved a step away but he came back, shot her a cocky grin and saluted. "My middle name is careful. Now, call 9-1-1 and get me some help." He started to shut the door but leaned back in. "I love you."

Then he was gone, running full tilt toward the inferno.

With shaking fingers, Cassidy punched in the numbers, reported the blaze and then turned to press her face against the side window, hoping and praying to see Nic return.

The fire was young but growing. An eerie golden glow shone through a window on one side of the house.

She saw Nic running around the structure, pounding on windows and doors, his voice raised in alarm. He disappeared around back and then reappeared on the front porch, pounding and yelling. To her horror, he shouldered the front door open and disappeared inside. Smoke gushed out like fog beneath the streetlights.

To hold back the cries of despair, Cassidy's hands pressed against her mouth.

"Oh, God in Heaven," she begged. "Protect him."

A litany of prayers pouring from her lips and heart, she rolled down the passenger window and coughed when smoke seeped across the lawn and into her lungs. How much worse must conditions be for Nic inside the house? She shuddered and turned to stare down the street, but all she saw were darkened homes and a few cars moving parallel to the quiet neighborhood.

Where was that fire engine? Why weren't they here?

Most importantly, where was Nic?

Mouth dry as sandpaper, she watched in terror as the blaze grew in power, like a beast fueled by all it devoured. A windowpane popped. Glass shattered.

Cassidy gripped the door handle.

In the next moment, she was standing on the grass, outside the truck, the stench of smoke thick and acrid.

Nic was in there. Her Nic.

Suddenly, one side of the roof leaned. A crash echoed across the yard.

Cassidy jerked, her horrified gasp the only human sound in the empty, lonely darkness. A terrible certainty washed over her in waves that left her shaking. If the roof had caved, Nic could be trapped.

In her memory, she was transported back to two unspeakable days beneath bricks and dirt, waiting for the unseen flames to claim her. Dear Lord, please don't let that happen to Nic. Please don't take him, too.

The fire spread, glowing in several windows now, but the man she loved did not return. What if the blaze had already overtaken him?

"No!" she screamed. Galvanizing anger ripped through her. With strength she didn't know she possessed, Cassidy's wobbly legs began to churn. They propelled her across the grass and toward the inferno. She would not let Nic die. She would not let fire steal someone else she loved.

Her feet hit the porch and thick smoke boiled as she charged through the door. A wall of heat slammed into her, scorching her lungs, sucking away her air.

In the distant night, sirens screamed, too far away. They wouldn't get here in time. She was the only one available to help Nic. She was the only one who could save him from the monster.

*Please help me, Lord. Help me be brave. Help me find him.*

Dozens of half-memorized scriptures flowed into her smoke-fogged mind. She grasped onto each one as if holding on to sanity.

*Even in the shadow of death, I will fear no evil for He is with me. He is my fortress and strong tower. Even if I walk through a fire, the Lord God of Israel, the Holy One, is with me. God is with me. God is with me.*

A beam crashed in front of her. She screamed and jumped back. Sparks shot out, burning her arms.

With a sob, she turned, trying to get her bearings. The gray smoke was everywhere and growing darker by the minute.

Where could Nic be?

A dog barked. She started in that direction. From somewhere she heard the crackle of fire but could see little other than thick, stinking smoke—just like in the Philippines.

She had charged into her worst nightmare.

"Nic! Where are you? Nic?" She screamed until the smoke stole her voice, refusing to be driven back by the crawling, clawing terror. Nic was in here somewhere. She wouldn't leave without him.


Nic jogged toward the curb to wait as Engine Four turned onto the street, lights and sirens in Code Three, and headed toward the burning house. The blast of noise brought people from their safe homes to gawk in curiosity. Nic paid them no mind.

From his cursory search, the blazing structure appeared empty, though for a minute there he'd been convinced he'd heard a voice.

The fire engine was still a couple of minutes away so he made his way to his truck to reassure Cassidy that all was well. Though she'd been terrified, he'd had no choice but to go against her wishes. With a heavy heart, he figured his decision was the final nail in the coffin of their relationship. He'd proven to her that he'd put himself in danger for someone else's benefit. This was who he was and what he did. He was finally proud of that, a pride Cassidy couldn't share. No amount of talking would change her mind now.

As he approached the vehicle, Nic slowed, squinting

through the darkness. Then he froze. His heart ricocheted against his rib cage.

Cassidy was not inside the truck.

Whirling, he searched the area. Her pale hair would be easy to spot, even at night.

"Cassidy?" he called, pulse starting to race in an ominous manner. He looked toward the dwelling. No way. She wouldn't have gone in there. She was too afraid.

The truth slapped him in the face. When the roof rumbled, he'd escaped through a side door. She hadn't seen him exit.

His knees went weak.

"Oh God," he breathed the prayer. Cassidy was in there. He knew that with a certainty he could not explain.

He started to run. From behind him shouts went up. "Stay back! Stay back!"

The fire truck was still a block away.

"There's a woman inside," he yelled as his feet clattered onto the porch.

Sirens screamed closer but not close enough.

Praying as he'd never prayed before, Nic flung himself into the inferno.

# Chapter Fifteen

Cassidy was lost. Total blackness encompassed her. She gagged at the stench of smoke everywhere.

Tears streamed down her face. Her eyes burned so badly she could barely keep them open. Even with her shirtsleeve over her mouth, rasping gasps issued from her throat.

She was in big trouble.

Vague memories of elementary school programs flickered in her head.

Smoke rose. Get down low. She went to her knees and then lower, pressing her face to the cooler, hard-surfaced floor. Better, but not much. Her heart pounded hard and fast, pleading for air. Belly crawling, she felt around her for a landmark of some kind to guide her out.

Her lungs screamed.

"Nic!" she called again.

Her head hurt, spinning with a gray fog as thick as the smoke. She couldn't be sure where the dizziness ended and the smoke began.

"Nic," she cried, though the effort cost her.

He was here somewhere, trapped and alone. She had to

save him. No more deaths. The room faded. She struggled to keep moving, her limbs heavier and heavier.

*God is with me. God is with me.*

She pressed her cheek against the floor to rest. A momentary reprieve. Only for minute. A minute's rest.

Outward sound ceased. The sound inside her head roared loudly.

*God is with me. I will not fear.*

Peace flowed through her like cool water.

Then all went dark.

Nic wasn't worried about losing his life, but he thought he might lose his mind.

Cassidy, that crazy, brave, incredible woman, was in here somewhere, facing the beast because of him.

He yanked his shirt over his nose and mouth and hit the floor, crawling on all fours through the acrid smoke. For the moment, the flames appeared confined to the kitchen to his left, but smoke filled the residence. Whatever had started the blaze had smoldered for a while.

"Cassidy! Where are you? Talk to me, Cass."

He was certain he'd heard her calling his name from this direction. "Cass."

No answer.

Prickles of fear crawled over his skin. He fought them off. Panic used precious air.

*Pray, Mama,* he thought, *and this time I'll pray, too.*

*God, you know where she is. Show me. Not for me. For her. For baby Alex.*

She'd come in here to rescue him. He could barely wrap his mind around that precious, foolish act.

With rigid discipline that would impress his chief, he kept

moving, searching along walls, sweeping his arms toward the center, praying every minute for contact.

Time was passing, seconds or minutes, he wasn't sure which. Little time remained before the smoke would be too much. Already tears streamed down his cheeks. His eyes burned ferociously.

*One more pass, Lord. Give me strength.*

"Cassidy!" he called, expecting nothing but hoping with all his being.

The sweetest sound echoed back, weak and raspy, a mere whimper, but close. "Nic."

From out of the smoke and darkness, Cassidy fell toward him. His heart surged. He gripped her arm. It was her. It was really her.

"Thank you, Lord," he croaked and felt Cassidy's answering nod. To her, he whispered, "Let's get out of here."

Upon entry, he'd mentally marked his escape route. Now, he began to backtrack, tugging Cassidy with him. Outside he could hear the calls of his fellow firefighters doing their jobs. A spray of water pummeled the side of the house.

A window popped. He heard glass shatter. Cassidy jerked. Her ragged breathing had worsened. She coughed.

Nic could take no more. Sucking in the thin air near the floor, he stood, pulling Cassidy up with him. Light beckoned to his right. Chest bursting, he swept her into his arms and raced toward what he hoped was a door.

Stumbling out onto the grass, Nic fell to his knees with Cassidy in his arms. Shouts went up from the bystanders. Footsteps pounded the grass. People ran toward them.

Sucking in great gulps of fresh night air, Nic tenderly cradled Cassidy against his chest. Gratitude welled inside him to the point of overflowing. They were safe. *She* was safe.

He gazed down at the woman he loved, the woman who'd

faced death to save him. Emergency lights rotated like strobes, bathing Cassidy's soot-covered skin in alternates of red and blue and white. Nic thought she'd never been more beautiful.

Still fighting for breath, he stroked back her tangled hair and pressed his lips to her forehead. Her eyes fluttered open and then closed again. The knot below Nic's rib cage tightened.

Paramedics, rattling with gear, reached his side.

"I'm okay," Nic said, waving away the woman with a stethoscope. His smoke-scourged voice sounded rough but he'd live. Cassidy was the one who mattered. "Take care of Cassidy."

Cassidy's eyes flew open, wildly seeking his face. Her fingers clutched his shirt. "No. I'm fine. Nic."

She struggled weakly against him as though she wanted to stand. Knowing how impossible that was, Nic held tight. "Shh. It's okay now. You're safe. We're both safe."

The reassurance seemed to be what she needed because she went limp, unresisting.

"We got her, Carano." Strong arms lifted her from him. It was all Nic could do to let her go. He remained on his knees on the grass, watching with heartfelt thanks as the paramedics placed Cassidy on a gurney and administered oxygen.

His head reeled with what had occurred this night. Cassidy had almost died because she'd thought he was inside a collapsing house. She'd faced her greatest fear for his sake. The impact of that silent statement filled him with wonder. He closed his eyes and sucked in more of the precious clean air.

*I love her, Lord. I don't want to lose her. Show me what to do now.*

Someone clapped a hand on his back. He looked up into the sculpted face of Sam Ridge. "Good job, buddy."

Sam had no idea that this incident had been his fault. If not for him, Cassidy would never have gone inside that house.

Hands on his thighs, Nic kept his gaze trained on Cassidy. "She's the hero."

Sam, in bunker gear, pivoted toward the ambulance. His reflective stripes glowed in the half-light, giving him an eerie quality. "That your woman?"

Reality dropped down upon Nic heavier than a boulder. Cassidy would never be his woman. Not now. If he'd had any hope at all to see her free of fear, tonight had stolen the last chance once and forever.

As the ambulance pulled away with Cassidy and his heart inside, Nic dropped his head. "Not anymore, Sam. Not anymore."

Cassidy was treated and released from the hospital, anxiously insisting on getting home to Alex. The teenagers had been worried, certain something had happened, but her baby boy had slept through it all.

"Are you sure you're all right, Cassidy?" Angie asked, her thin face worried.

Cassidy swallowed, throat raw. "I will be, but thanks for spending the night."

The teen shrugged. "No problem. Is there anything I can do for you?"

Cassidy stood at Alex's crib, filthy and stinking of smoke. Her head hurt, but her heart hurt more. At the emergency room, she'd hoped for a chance to talk to Nic, but he'd never appeared.

She supposed he'd finally gotten the message that she didn't want him in her life.

"I'm such a coward," she whispered.

"Huh?" Angie shifted toward her, stirring the scent of her recent shower and Cassidy's borrowed shampoo.

"Nothing. Talking to myself."

"About Nic?"

She turned incredulous eyes on the fresh-scrubbed teen. "How did you know?"

Angie shrugged, a sly smile spreading over her lips. "If I had a guy like that, I would talk to myself all the time."

The comment amused Cassidy. "I admit to being a blubbering idiot, but that wasn't what I meant."

"I know. I was kidding. What gives with you two anyway?"

"Nothing."

"Do you love him?"

Discussing Nic with a fifteen-year-old seemed ridiculous, but Angie and the other girls had poured their hearts out to her more times than she could count. "I do."

"So what's the issue?"

Teenagers saw everything in black and white. They thought love was the answer to everything. If you loved a guy, that was enough. Cassidy knew better.

"I messed everything up." Cassidy raised a hand to her forehead, rubbing the ache between her eyebrows. "The situation is too complicated."

Angie made a rude sound of disbelief. "Don't be a dill weed, Cassidy. The guy is a hunk. He's crazy in love with you. Do something about it."

"If only the solution was that easy."

Angie tilted her head as if certain Cassidy was off-center. Maybe she was.

The mistakes had been hers. The problem was hers. Maybe the solution *was* that easy.

She spun toward Angie, headache suddenly unimportant. "Would you mind keeping an eye on Alex while I run downstairs?"

Angie pointed a hot-pink fingernail at the doorway. "Go. Now."

She was still grinning when Cassidy rushed out the door.

\* \* \*

Somebody was knocking.

Nic struggled up from sleep. A tune played in his head. "Somebody's knocking, should I let 'em in?"

He chuckled and snuggled his face into the soft leather. When he'd arrived home, he'd collapsed in the recliner, too tired and distressed to undress. He must have fallen asleep instantly.

The pounding came again.

With a growl, he struggled to sit up. The old recliner squeaked into an upright position.

Somebody *was* knocking.

Curious but seriously dead-headed, he staggered to the door and wrenched it open.

A gray-faced version of Cassidy spoke in a scratchy whisper. "I was wrong."

He stared for two beats. Nah, couldn't be. He must still be asleep. He closed the door and stumbled back toward the recliner. Halfway there, he stopped. He rubbed a hand down his face, shook the cobwebs out. His hands stunk of smoke. Oh man. He wasn't asleep.

"Cassidy?" he said to the dark room.

His heart jump-started. Spinning so fast his head swam, Nic yanked the door open again. She was still there. He wilted against the jamb. "I thought you were a dream."

"I know it's late. Maybe I should have waited until tomorrow, but—" She stopped and bit down on that fascinating bottom lip.

Nic reached out and snagged her arm. "Get in here."

She obeyed. Fancy that.

"Did I wake you?"

"Nah." He tripped over his shoes. "Well, actually yes, but it's all good. What's up?"

He snapped on a lamp. A yellow cone of light flooded the floor, leaving the perimeter in shadows.

Cassidy fidgeted, twisting her hands in front of her. "I need to talk to you."

Right. Been there, done that. Still had the gaping wound in his chest. "We talked already. You gave me the boot."

Keep it light and breezy, Carano. One heart-stomping in twenty-four hours is enough for anyone.

"Can I take it back?"

He blinked, then scratched the back of his head. "Am I still asleep?"

"I hope not." She took a step. Approximately three feet separated them but she was definitely moving into his space. He didn't want to be happy about that but what could he do? He was a sucker for the woman upstairs.

"Nic." She twisted her hands again. "I love you."

Yeah, yeah, she'd said that before. "You said love wasn't enough."

"Maybe it's not."

"Right." He took a step away from her.

Cassidy moved forward. "Hear me out, please. I've only got so much throat left."

The raspy words reminded him of their night's work. Chastened, he said, "Are you all right? What did the doctors say?"

She waved him off. "Stop it, Nic. Let me say this. I love you. I love everything about you. Tonight when I thought you might die, I…"

Tears sprang to her eyes. She turned her head, trying to hide them.

That's all it took. Nic crossed the space between them in one second flat to cup her face. "You came in after me. Why? Why did you do such a foolish thing?"

Her hot tears fell onto his fingers. She lifted her chin. "Because I love you. I need you in my life. Alex needs you."

Though he'd kick himself tomorrow, Nic tilted her head

and kissed the tears from her cheeks. "You are the most confusing woman but I love you anyway. I just wish…"

"What?" she whispered. "What do you wish?"

"I wish you weren't afraid. I wish you could accept me for the man I am. I wish we could be together." He dropped his hand, furious at the ache in his voice. She'd already made herself clear on the topic.

"Nic, that's what I'm trying to tell you." She grabbed his hand and held on tight. "Tonight something happened to me inside that house. I felt God's presence in a way I can't explain. And as I stumbled through the smoke, praying for you, begging God to spare your life, I realized something very important."

"What was it?"

"I'm not afraid anymore. Inside that house, the most perfect peace settled over me. For the first time since I was a little girl, I knew I could trust God with my life. And with my love. He sent you along to teach me that and to set me free."

Nic was so stunned he couldn't speak.

Cassidy's beautiful, smudged face twisted in worry. "Can you forgive me? Can we start again? Please say I'm not too late."

All he could think of was, "This is a dream. I should lie down."

Cassidy moved closer. Sliding her arms around his waist, she stared up into his face. His heart chugged like a steam engine. Her blue, blue eyes melted him, boring into him, making promises he wanted her to keep. He knew then, knew without a shadow of a doubt, that Cassidy meant exactly what she said.

But he had to hear her say it. "You choose me? Fire helmet and all?"

She nodded. "I do, if you'll have me."

As if the weight of the earth had been lifted from his shoulders, Nic closed his eyes and rejoiced. "I love you, Cassidy."

Her eyes twinkled up at him. "More than Mandy and Rachel and all those others?"

He did his best to appear obtuse. "Who?"

She tiptoed up and bit his chin. "You heard me."

"Ouch. Wicked woman." Then all frivolity disappeared. "I've been looking for you all my life."

"Same here," she murmured. This time she kissed his chin.

"Much better." He smiled into her eyes. "But higher would be stupendously better."

Cassidy's beautiful mouth curved and moved closer. "I think," she whispered, "that's an excellent idea."

# Epilogue

Fire Station One seemed unusually quiet as Cassidy pulled into the visitor's parking space, unharnessed Alex and went inside. She stopped in the doorway to listen. Cool air rushed at her, but the usual bustle and murmur of men at work was missing.

Rounding the small kitchen/living area, she headed down the hall past the offices and out toward the truck bay. Three trucks—the engine, the brush pumper and the air truck—were parked side by side as always, gleaming clean and ready to roll at the sound of an alarm. As she approached the double glass door leading out into the bay, a firefighter disappeared between the engine and brush pumper.

In the two months since the fire, Cassidy had found a new freedom as well as newfound happiness. Facing her fears head-on, she now visited the fire station to share lunch with Nic every time he was on duty. Though the other firefighters teased him about losing all his other girlfriends, Nic didn't seem to mind. The more she learned about him and about his selfless work, the more she fell in love with Nic Carano. He was no longer Notorious Nic, the shallow ladies' man with no substance.

"Nic?" The heels of her sandals sounded hollow in the cavernous bay. "Sam?"

As if he'd been waiting for her voice, Sam Ridge appeared from the space between the two trucks. His expressionless face looked darker than usual. Was the man blushing? "Nic's over here. Come on around."

Those were more words than she'd ever heard the Kiowa say at once. Hoisting a babbling, bouncing Alex higher on one hip, Cassidy followed Sam's order.

As she rounded the front of the massive truck, the sight stopped her in her tracks. A dozen firefighters, a smattering of her and Nic's friends, the Carano family and even her grandmother stood around a white linen–covered table.

Bewildered, Cassidy looked at the grinning faces. "What's going on?"

Nic, looking crisp and handsome in dress blues, stepped from behind the gathering and strode toward her. The *tap-tap* of his black shoes matched the rhythm of her heart. Intensely dark eyes latched onto hers and wouldn't let go. She knew him well enough to see his nerves, though others wouldn't notice the rapid rise and fall of his chest or the way his nostrils flared the tiniest bit.

"Nic?" What was going on?

He took Alex from her arms, handing the baby off to his sister. Then he shocked her silent when he took her hand and dropped to one knee.

"Cassidy Luanne Willis." He stopped and cleared his throat. Someone—Adam, she thought—chuckled. "When God brought you into my life, I was a mess. I didn't know it, but I was. I'd been running from God, running from my family." One shoulder rose and fell. "Just running in general, like a lost pup. Then you and Alex came along and suddenly the whole world took on new meaning."

Cassidy touched his cheek with trembling fingers. She smiled, felt her lips trembling, too, and her eyes growing moist. Was he about to propose? Here? In front of all these people?

She opened her mouth to speak but closed it again when Nic reached into his pocket and removed a black velvet ring box. When he flipped up the lid, Cassidy gasped at the stunning engagement ring inside.

"I love you, Cassidy. And I love that little boy over there. What I'm trying to say is this." His fingers shook as he removed the diamond solitaire. "Will you marry me? Will you do me the honor of being my wife?"

He slid the ring onto her third finger. Cassidy stared at her hand in stunned joy and then at the man she loved with everything inside her.

She didn't hesitate a second.

"Yes!" she screamed. "Yes!"

Her knees gave way then and she tumbled down, falling against Nic's sturdy form. His strong, firefighter arms circled around her, holding her safe. She could feel him trembling, too, and was humbled by the power and beauty of his love.

The tears she'd been holding back fell like rain. She buried her face in Nic's shoulder and sobbed.

In the next moment, they were surrounded by well-wishers. Voices rose and fell in laughter and congratulations. Cameras flashed.

With Nic's hand rubbing soothing circles on her back and his amused voice whispering sweet things in her ear, Cassidy finally hiccuped away the joyful sobs. Together they stood, Nic's arm firmly around her waist, snugging her to his side, right where she wanted to be.

He leaned to whisper against her hair. "I love you. Do you like my surprise?"

Through a watery smile she beamed up at him. "I love your surprise. But I love you more."

He patted his chest twice. "That's what I'm talking about right there. Come on. There's cake."

"From Carano's Bakery?"

"Where else? The best Italian cream cake on the planet."

Cassidy groaned in mock dismay. "I'll never fit into a wedding dress."

Her grandmother, dressed in pumps and a blue business suit, approached with her usual no-nonsense bossiness. "Cassidy, we need to talk."

Cassidy fought not to let the woman ruin her wonderful engagement party.

"Thank you for being here, Grandmother," she said, hoping to circumvent any unpleasant remarks. "It means a lot to me."

"Of course I'd be here. You're my only granddaughter." Eleanor sniffed and Cassidy was astonished to see tears glistening in her eyes. "Apparently this young man loves you. He seems to be solvent, a man of character, and he's gone to a great deal of trouble to make this surprise engagement party work. You'll do well with him."

Cassidy was too stunned for words. Grandmother approved? She had never approved of anything Cassidy did. Cassidy turned her head the slightest bit to stare at Nic in wonder. Amusement twinkled from his eyes. He winked. Somehow he'd worked his charm on Eleanor Bassett.

"Now," Grandmother said, returning the attention to herself. "The two of you need to adopt Alex. A child needs two parents. I've already discussed the issue with my attorney. He'll take care of everything, paid in full. Just call him."

Though barely able to believe her ears, Cassidy was deeply touched. For once, Grandmother's bossiness did not offend. "Thank you, Grandmother. This means more than I can say."

"Well." Awkwardly, Eleanor patted her on the shoulder. "I think I'll have some punch."

With the regal posture of a queen, she moved toward the table where Captain Summers dipped golden punch into clear cups and Gabe Carano slid sandwiches onto paper plates. Next to him, his wife cut perfect slivers of Italian cream cake. Nic's father, Leo, captured all the proceedings on video, his balding head shiny with perspiration.

"I thought about pizza," Nic said.

"This is perfect. Perfect."

"Yeah," he said happily. "I think so, too."

He led her to the circle of folding chairs where several children, women and firefighters were gathered. He bent to kiss his mother on the cheek. "Doing okay?"

Although dark circles rimmed the eyes so like her son's, Rosalie touched Nic's cheek and beamed. "Happiest day I've had in months."

The words were true and a painful reminder that the Carano family faced struggles of their own. Yet, their faith and love sustained them. Cassidy vowed to remember and to continue that legacy in her own family. Hers and Nic's.

"Come on, you two, kiss for the camera." Nic's brother Adam pointed a digital in their direction.

Nic laughed and pumped his dark eyebrows. "I can handle that."

As he bent to kiss her, the fire alarm began to wail. Nic jerked upright. The other firefighters were already in motion, running toward the engine.

"Sorry, sweetheart. I gotta go." He kissed her nose.

"I know. It's fine. Go." And she told the truth. Fear no longer ruled her life. "I'll be here when you return."

He hesitated, fingers on her face. "You're really okay?"

She smiled, heart full. "I really am."

He stared at her for one more second. "I love you."

"And I love you with everything I am and all that I'll ever have. You are my hero."

"You're mine, too," he whispered, bending to press his lips to hers. Though the kiss was brief, she felt the love all the way to her toes.

As she watched her firefighter dive into the open door of the truck, heard the doors slam and watched the shiny red engine roll into traffic, horns and lights blaring, a beautiful, joyous peace flowed over her. God never promised that life would be without heartache but He'd promised to always be there to comfort, love and heal.

With His help, Cassidy had walked through the fire and come out stronger. She fully trusted that her hero would always do the same.

An arm went around her shoulders from the left, and then another from the right. She looked up to find herself bracketed by Adam and Gabe. In the next instant, she was surrounded by Caranos, stalwart and faithful and supportive.

Struck with awe, Cassidy could almost hear God whispering in her ear.

For as long as she could remember, she'd longed for a big loving family. Now, here they were, full of smiles and laughter and love, eager to welcome her into the fold.

\* \* \* \* \*

Dear Reader,

Ideas for books come about in a variety of ways. Sometimes I get an idea from an incident in real life or from a song or a single turn of phrase that tickles my fancy. Sometimes an idea arrives like a gift. This is what happened to me with *The Baby Bond*. About the same time I began brainstorming ideas for my next Love Inspired, my grandson was born. A few days after Noah's birth, my son sent a photo of the new baby. Since my son, the baby's daddy, is a firefighter, the photographer had the brilliant notion to place the newborn inside my son's upturned helmet. The moment I saw that precious photo that spoke of the love of a firefighter for a baby boy, the wheels began to turn inside my head. What if a firefighter fell in love with an orphaned baby he rescued from a burning house? In a short time, the idea for *The Baby Bond* came to be.

I truly hope you've enjoyed the story. I love hearing from readers so feel free to write me c/o Steeple Hill, 233 Broadway, Suite 1001, New York, NY 10279 or through my Web site at www.lindagoodnight.com

Warmly,

Linda Goodnight

# QUESTIONS FOR DISCUSSION

1. Name the main characters. Who was your favorite? Why?

2. Could you relate to any of the characters in the book? How?

3. What incident drew Cassidy and Nic together?

4. Although a Christian, Cassidy was riddled with fear. What was she afraid of? Why?

5. Do you think Cassidy's fears were realistic? Is it possible to be so afraid that fear interferes with a person's life choices? Have you ever known anyone like that?

6. How can someone overcome great fear? Do you believe facing a fear will make it better or worse? How can faith help a person deal with fear?

7. Cassidy says someone told her that fear is the opposite of faith. Rather than helping, the statement hurt her. Why? Have you ever been told you didn't have enough faith? How did it make you feel?

8. Nic felt pressured by his family. In what way? Were his feelings justified? Explain.

9. Have you ever struggled under family expectations? In what way? How did you handle the issues?

10. Some people believe that everything happens for a reason. Do you? Can you find scripture to back up your opinion?

11. When Cassidy chose to raise her orphaned nephew, her grandmother fought against the decision. Why?

12. Nic's brothers claimed he slid by on his parents' prayers. What does that mean? Is such a thing scripturally possible? What does the Bible say about the power of a praying parent?

13. Scripture says that love will cast out fear. How does this relate to what Cassidy did at the end of the book?

When her neighbor proposes a "practical" marriage, romantic Rene Mitchell throws the ring in his face. Fleeing Texas for Montana, Rene rides with trucker Clay Preston—and rescues an expectant mother stranded in a snowstorm. Clay doesn't believe in romance, but can Rene change his mind?

*Turn the page for a sneak preview of*
*"A Dry Creek Wedding"*
*by Janet Tronstad,*
*one of the heartwarming stories about wedded bliss*
*in the new collection*
*SMALL-TOWN BRIDES.*
*Available in June 2009 from Love Inspired®.*

"Never let your man go off by himself in a snow storm," Mandy said. The inside of the truck's cab was dark except for a small light on the ceiling. "I should have stopped my Davy."

"I doubt you could have," Rene said as she opened her left arm to hug the young woman. "Not if he thought you needed help. Here, put your head on me. You may as well stretch out as much as you can until Clay gets back."

Mandy put her head on Rene's shoulder. "He's going to marry you some day, you know."

"Who?" Rene adjusted the blankets as Mandy stretched out her legs.

"A rodeo man would make a good husband," Mandy muttered as she turned slightly and arched her back.

"Clay? He doesn't even believe in love."

Well, that got Mandy's attention, Rene thought, as the younger woman looked up at her and frowned. "Really?"

Rene nodded.

"Well, you have to have love," Mandy said firmly. "Even my Davy says he loves me. It's important."

"I know." Rene wondered how her life had ever gotten so turned around. A few days ago she thought Trace was her destiny and now she was kissing a man who would rather order up a wife from some catalogue than actually fall in love. She'd felt the kiss he'd given her more deeply than she should, too. Which meant she needed to get back on track.

"I'm going to make a list," Rene said. "Of all the things I need in a husband. That's how I'll know when I find the right one."

Mandy drew in her breath. "I can help. For you, not for me. I want my Davy."

Rene looked out the side window and saw that the light was coming back to the truck. She motioned for Mandy to sit up again. She doubted Clay had found Mandy's boyfriend. She'd have to keep the young woman distracted for a little bit longer.

Clay took his hat off before he opened the door to his truck. Then he brushed his coat before climbing inside. He didn't want to scatter snow all over the women.

"Did you see him?" Mandy asked quietly from the middle of the seat.

Clay shook his head. "I'll need to come back."

"But—" Mandy protested until another pain caught her and she drew in her breath.

"It won't take long to get you to Dry Creek," Clay said as he started his truck. "Then I can come back and look some more."

Clay didn't like leaving the man out there any more than Mandy did, but it could take hours to find him, and the sooner they got Mandy comfortable and relaxed, the sooner those labor pains of hers would go away.

"I feel a lot better," Mandy said. "If you'd just go back and look some more, I'll be fine."

Clay looked at the young woman as she bit her bottom lip. Mandy was in obvious pain regardless of what she said. "You're not fine, and there's no use pretending."

Mandy gasped, half in indignation this time.

Those pains worried him, but he assumed she must know the difference between the ones she was having and ones that signaled the baby was coming. Women went to class for that kind of thing these days. She probably just needed to lie down somewhere and put her feet up.

"He's right," Rene said as she put her hand on Mandy's stomach. "Davy wouldn't want you out here. He'll tell you that when we find him. And think of the baby."

Mandy turned to look at Rene and then looked back at Clay.

"You promise you'll come back?" Mandy asked. "Right away?"

"You have my word," Clay said as he started to back up the truck.

"That should be on your list," Mandy said as she looked up at Rene. "Number one—he needs to keep his word."

Clay wondered if the two women were still talking about the baby Mandy was having. It seemed a bit premature to worry about the little guy's character, but he was glad to see that the young woman had something to occupy her mind. Maybe she had plans for her baby to grow up to be president or something.

"I don't know," Rene muttered. "We can talk about it later."

"We've got some time," Clay said. "It'll take us fifteen minutes at least to get to Dry Creek. You may as well make your list."

Mandy shifted on the seat again. "So, you think trust is important in a husband?"

"A *husband?*" Clay almost missed the turn. "You're making a list for a husband?"

"Well, not for me," Mandy said patiently. "It's Rene's list, of course."

Clay grunted. Of course.

"He should be handsome, too," Mandy added as she stretched. "But maybe not smooth, if you know what I mean. Rugged, like a man, but nice."

Clay could feel Mandy's eyes on him.

"I don't really think I need a list," Rene said so low Clay could barely hear her.

Clay didn't know why he was so annoyed that Rene was making a list. "Just don't put Trace's name on that thing."

"I'm not going to put anyone's name on it," Rene said as she sat up straighter. "And you're the one who doesn't think people should just fall in love. I'd think you would *like* a list."

Clay had to admit she had a point. He should be in favor of a list like that; it eliminated feelings. It must be all this stress that was making him short-tempered. "If you're going to have a list, you may as well make the guy rich."

That should show he was able to join into the spirit of the thing.

"There's no need to ridicule—" Rene began.

"A good job does help," Mandy interrupted solemnly. "Especially when you start having babies. I'm hoping the job in Idaho pays well. We need a lot of things to set up our home."

"You should make a list of what you need for your house," Clay said encouragingly. Maybe the women would talk about clocks and chairs instead of husbands. He'd seen enough of life to know there were no fairy tale endings. Not in his life.

\* \* \* \* \*

*Will spirited Rene Mitchell change trucker Clay Preston's*
*mind about love?*
*Find out in*
SMALL-TOWN BRIDES,
*the heartwarming anthology from*
*beloved authors Janet Tronstad and Debra Clopton.*
*Available in June 2009 from Love Inspired®*

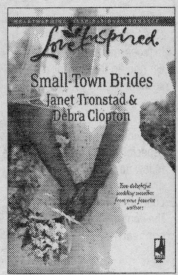

# REQUEST YOUR FREE BOOKS!

## 2 FREE INSPIRATIONAL NOVELS
## PLUS 2
## FREE
## MYSTERY GIFTS

*Love Inspired.*

**YES!** Please send me 2 FREE Love Inspired® novels and my 2 FREE mystery gifts (gifts are worth about $10). After receiving them, if I don't wish to receive any more books, I can return the shipping statement marked "cancel". If I don't cancel, I will receive 4 brand-new novels every month and be billed just $4.24 per book in the U.S. or $4.74 per book in Canada, plus 25¢ shipping and handling per book and applicable taxes, if any*. That's a savings of over 20% off the cover price! I understand that accepting the 2 free books and gifts places me under no obligation to buy anything. I can always return a shipment and cancel at any time. Even if I never buy another book, the two free books and gifts are mine to keep forever.

113 IDN ERXA  313 IDN ERWX

| | |
|---|---|
| Name | (PLEASE PRINT) |

| | |
|---|---|
| Address | Apt. # |

| | | |
|---|---|---|
| City | State/Prov. | Zip/Postal Code |

Signature (if under 18, a parent or guardian must sign)

### Order online at www.LoveInspiredBooks.com

### Or mail to Steeple Hill Reader Service:

**IN U.S.A.:** P.O. Box 1867, Buffalo, NY  14240-1867
**IN CANADA:** P.O. Box 609, Fort Erie, Ontario  L2A 5X3

Not valid to current subscribers of Love Inspired books.

### Want to try two free books from another series?
### Call 1-800-873-8635 or visit www.morefreebooks.com

* Terms and prices subject to change without notice. N.Y. residents add applicable sales tax. Canadian residents will be charged applicable provincial taxes and GST. Offer not valid in Quebec. This offer is limited to one order per household. All orders subject to approval. Credit or debit balances in a customer's account(s) may be offset by any other outstanding balance owed by or to the customer. Please allow 4 to 6 weeks for delivery. Offer available while quantities last.

LIREG08R